W9-AMY-873

THE BOBBSEY TWINS

AND THE PLAY HOUSE SECRET

TREASURES FOR SALE!

Bert and Nan Bobbsey answer this ad and buy a Valentine surprise for Freddie and Flossie. After the gift is hidden, strange noises are heard in the attic. Meanwhile Nan has discovered a play house behind a nearby mansion. Scary things happen in the little house. Who is trying to frighten the twins away, and why? Is the secret in the big locked closet?

Through it all, Mr. and Mrs. Bobbsey are away, and lovable old Aunt Sallie is in charge—until she becomes ill. Laughs and chills chase each other as the snowbound children keep house with a spook in the attic! Excitement mounts to a thrilling finish when the twins and their friends have a Valentine party, solve this mystery, and uncover the play house secret all on the same day!

THE BOBBSEY TWINS

By Laura Lee Hope

THE BOBBSEY TWINS OF LAKEPORT
ADVENTURE IN THE COUNTRY
THE SECRET AT THE SEASHORE
MYSTERY AT SCHOOL
AND THE MYSTERY AT SNOW LODGE
ON A HOUSEBOAT
MYSTERY AT MEADOWBROOK
BIG ADVENTURE AT HOME
SEARCH IN THE GREAT CITY
ON BLUEBERRY ISLAND
MYSTERY ON THE DEEP BLUE SEA
ADVENTURE IN WASHINGTON
VISIT TO THE GREAT WEST
AND THE CEDAR CAMP MYSTERY
AND THE COUNTY FAIR MYSTERY
CAMPING OUT
ADVENTURES WITH BABY MAY
AND THE PLAY HOUSE SECRET
AND THE FOUR-LEAF CLOVER MYSTERY
WONDERFUL WINTER SECRET
AND THE CIRCUS SURPRISE
SOLVE A MYSTERY
IN THE LAND OF COTTON
AT MYSTERY MANSION
IN TULIP LAND
IN RAINBOW VALLEY
OWN LITTLE RAILROAD
AT WHITESAIL HARBOR
AND THE HORSESHOE RIDDLE
AT BIG BEAR POND
ON A BICYCLE TRIP
OWN LITTLE FERRYBOAT
AT PILGRIM ROCK
FOREST ADVENTURE
AT LONDON TOWER
IN THE MYSTERY CAVE
IN VOLCANO LAND
THE GOLDFISH MYSTERY
AND THE BIG RIVER MYSTERY
AND THE GREEK HAT MYSTERY
SEARCH FOR THE GREEN ROOSTER
AND THEIR CAMEL ADVENTURE
MYSTERY OF THE KING'S PUPPET
AND THE SECRET OF CANDY CASTLE
AND THE DOODLEBUG MYSTERY

A big white thing rose flapping out of the trunk!

The Bobbsey Twins and the Play House Secret

By

LAURA LEE HOPE

GROSSET & DUNLAP
Publishers *New York*

ISBN: 0-448-08018-4

PRINTED IN THE UNITED STATES OF AMERICA
LIBRARY OF CONGRESS CATALOG CARD NO. 68-29947
The Bobbsey Twins and the Play House Secret

CONTENTS

THE BOBBSEY TWINS AND THE PLAY HOUSE SECRET

CHAPTER I

TREASURES

"FLOSSIE! Watch out!" Nan Bobbsey exclaimed.

A huge snarling dog had bounded from the yard the sisters were passing and leaped at the blond six-year-old.

"Help!" shrieked the little girl, holding a red envelope high in her mittened hand.

Nan, who was twelve, struck at the dog with one of her schoolbooks.

Just then the girls' two brothers dashed up. "Get away!" shouted Bert, Nan's twin. He swung his notebook at the dog.

Barking loudly, the dog raced off through the yard toward a large, gray stone house.

"What a mean dog!" exclaimed Freddie. He was Flossie's twin and was also blond and blue-eyed. Bert and Nan had dark hair and eyes.

"I wonder whose dog he is," said Bert. "Nobody has lived here in the Springer place for over a year."

"Look!" Nan gasped. "There's a face in the window!"

"Where? I don't see anyone," said Bert.

"On the second floor," Nan replied, pointing. "I just saw the curtain move, and somebody peeked out."

"Maybe the house has been sold," Bert remarked. "What did the face look like?"

"A man's," his sister replied, "but I couldn't see him very well."

As the children walked toward their home, the afternoon sun went behind the clouds. A sharp February wind whipped a pile of dry leaves across the yard.

Flossie clung to her red envelope. "Well, anyway, that horrid dog didn't hurt the s'prise I made in school today."

At the corner Nan paused. "You skip on home," she said to the younger twins. "Bert and I will be along soon."

"Where are you going?" Flossie asked.

"To see somebody," said Nan mysteriously.

"We'll go with you," Freddie offered.

"Not this time," Bert replied with a wink at Nan.

"Why can't we?" Flossie asked. "Is it a secret?"

"Yes, it is," Nan replied.

"Look!" Nan gasped. "There's a face in the window!"

"Oh, okay." Flossie sighed. She and Freddie walked on.

The older twins crossed the street and hurried down a side road to a white bungalow. A pencil-printed note was tacked to the front door: RING AND WALK IN. Bert pushed the bell, opened the door, and the children stepped into a dim hallway.

"Bert and Nan Bobbsey!" exclaimed a cheerful voice.

A tall woman in a flowered dress came through a door at the rear. She had short curly gray hair and a friendly smile. "Put your books on the little table and take off your coats."

"Mrs. Villey," said Nan, "we saw your ad in the paper—'Treasures for Sale.' "

"What are they?" Bert asked.

"I'll show you," Mrs. Villey replied and led the twins into a small living room.

"Wow!" exclaimed Bert, and Nan's eyes opened wide.

The room was crammed with pictures, statues, lamps, tapestries, clocks, and fancy dishes. Every chair and table had something on it, and the floor was crowded with boxes.

"I cleaned out my attic," said Mrs. Villey. "All my treasures must go! I'm moving to my daughter's home."

"They're lovely," Nan remarked. "Where did they come from?"

"India, China, France," Mrs. Villey answered. "When my husband was alive, we traveled a great deal." Then she added, "Where are Freddie and Flossie?"

Nan chuckled. "We wouldn't let them come. You see, we want to buy a Valentine surprise for them."

"How about this?" Bert asked. He stepped carefully into the crowded room and pointed to a bottle with a small ship in it.

Nan had spotted a little wooden house which seemed to be made of gingerbread. "What about that?" She pointed.

Mrs. Villey smiled, as the twins picked their way over to the little house. It was about as high as their knees and had two doors in the front. Outside one of the doors stood the figure of a witch.

Mrs. Villey explained that Hansel and Gretel were inside. "They come out the other door when the weather is going to be nice. Then the witch goes inside."

"But now she's out," said Nan. "Does that mean rain?"

"Yes. Or maybe snow."

Bert asked how much Mrs. Villey wanted for the toy. She told him, and the children said they would take it.

While Bert was paying for the curio, Nan looked over the other treasures. On a chair stood a little Chinese house made of thin bamboo sticks. It had a curved roof like a pagoda.

"What's this, Mrs. Villey?" she asked.

"A very old cage. It was made in the eighteenth century. I bought it in Hong Kong."

"Was it for birds?"

"No. Some Chinese child kept white mice in it."

"It's fascinating," said Nan. From each of the four corners of the roof hung a small gold bell. She flicked one carefully, and it tinkled.

"That's a real treasure," Mrs. Villey told them. "An antique dealer should be willing to give me a good price for it." Then she smiled. "Now that we've finished our business, how about a little snack?"

"Thanks. That would be great," Bert answered.

"Then come along," said Mrs. Villey. She led them down the hall and through the door into a cheerful, well-lighted kitchen.

While she and the children were enjoying cupcakes and cocoa, Bert said, "I have an idea! Let's play a little joke on Flossie and Freddie."

"How?" his sister asked.

"We'll tell each one that we have a surprise for the *other*."

Nan giggled. "That would be fun. I can just see their faces when they find out it's for both of them."

When Bert finished eating, he asked Mrs. Villey if he could wrap the gingerbread house.

"Don't bother," she replied. "It's awkward to carry. I've hired a man to deliver everything. He'll bring your gingerbread house in a day or two."

"All right," said Nan. "It would be better anyhow if Freddie and Flossie don't see us with a box."

Mrs. Villey took a small pad and pencil from her dress pocket. "Now give me your address," she said, then added, "Oh, I left my glasses on a little table in the living room."

"I'll get them," said Nan.

She hurried down the gloomy hall to the living room. It was so dim, she paused at the door, looking for the table where the glasses were.

Just then Nan heard a tinkling sound. She was not alone! A man was kneeling on the floor beside the bamboo cage, slipping something into his pocket.

"Hello," said Nan.

With a start he jumped up, bumping the chair.

"Be careful—the cage!" cried Nan as the bamboo house fell to the floor.

She hurried over and helped him pick up the curio. As they settled it on the chair, she saw that he looked very angry.

"What do you think you're doing," he asked

sharply, "sneaking up on a person like that?"

"I'm sorry," said Nan. "I didn't mean to scare you."

Mrs. Villey and Bert walked in. "I thought I heard something fall," Mrs. Villey said.

The man turned quickly and took off his hat. "Excuse me, madam," he said politely. "I'm afraid I was a bit clumsy."

Mrs. Villey switched on a lamp. They saw that the stranger was of medium height and had thin dark hair combed carefully over a bald spot. He smiled, but his dark eyes were not friendly.

"We didn't hear the bell ring," said Mrs. Villey.

"I rang it," the man said promptly. "Maybe I didn't push it hard enough."

"If you'll excuse me a moment, sir, I'll be right with you," Mrs. Villey said.

Nan spotted the glasses and handed them over to her. While Bert dictated the address, Mrs. Villey wrote it down on her pad. Then she turned over the paper and printed: SOLD TO THE BOBBSEYS.

"There now," she said. "I'll attach this to the gingerbread house."

The children thanked her, and she took them to the hall. They put on their coats, picked up their books, and said good-by.

Mrs. Villey hurried back to her customer and

the twins heard the man ask the price of the Chinese mouse cage.

As soon as the door was closed, Nan said, "Bert, is the doorbell hard to ring?"

"No. It's easy."

"Then I'll bet he didn't ring it," Nan said, when they reached the street. "You should have seen how scared he was—and mad, too. And he slipped something into his pocket."

"Maybe he was stealing the thing he put into his pocket," Bert suggested.

Nan nodded. "Perhaps he sneaked in hoping to pick up something. I'm glad I stopped him."

With the wind biting their faces, the children hurried toward their home. Suddenly they heard a shout and saw Freddie and Flossie playing in a lot with a half-built house on it. The twins were sliding on the ice in a long ditch that ran to a window opening in the cellar. At the window stood a large lighted red lantern.

"It's fun! Try it, Bert!" Freddie called out. "But don't go all the way to the lantern."

At this moment two big boys in hooded jackets came from among the trees behind the lot. They walked over to Freddie and Flossie, grinning.

"Oh-oh, here comes trouble," said Bert.

Danny Rugg and Jack Westley were his schoolmates, but he did not like them. They were always playing mean tricks on children smaller than themselves.

As Freddie took a running jump onto the slide, Danny gave him a hard push. With a yell Freddie fell flat on his back and slid along fast on the ice. The next moment he reached the end of the ditch.

Freddie and the lantern crashed through the window opening and dropped into the cellar!

CHAPTER II

SURPRISES

"FREDDIE!" screamed Flossie, covering her eyes with her hands.

Nan and Bert ran forward. They noticed that Danny and Jack had scooted off looking frightened.

When the twins reached the window opening, they peered inside. It was so dim in the cellar, Bert and Nan could see very little.

"Freddie!" they called.

"I'm here," he answered.

"Are you all right?" Nan asked.

"Yes. But look!"

At this instant Bert saw a flame near his brother. The lantern had set fire to a piece of paper!

In a flash Bert was through the window. He picked up the overturned lantern and hurled it outside. Nan now jumped down, and together they stamped out the fire.

"Freddie, you sure you're okay?" Nan asked her young brother.

"Sure," he insisted, "but I'd like to give that Danny Rugg a punch."

"You stay away from him," Bert ordered, as they helped Freddie climb out. "He's too big for you."

Flossie was so relieved to see her twin that she just stared at him.

"We'd better hurry home," said Nan, "or we'll miss Dinah and Sam."

Dinah and Sam Johnson were the good-natured Negro couple who worked for the Bobbseys and lived on the third floor of their house. As long as the children could remember, Dinah had been the family's housekeeper and her thin, friendly husband had worked in their father's lumberyard.

"I wish we were going South with them," said Freddie as the children hurried down the street.

"Let's stop in the Goody Shoppe and buy them a going-away present," Nan suggested.

Flossie nodded, then took the red envelope from her pocket and smoothed the paper. "Their card is ready," she said.

The children picked out a box of candy, then hurried home. When they walked in, their parents were in the front hall with Dinah and Sam. All of them had on coats and hats and were surrounded by suitcases.

Suddenly the children spied someone else. "Aunt Sallie!" they chorused, and hugged the small white-haired woman who stepped from behind their tall, handsome father.

"Surprise!" she said, smiling. "I've come to stay with you!"

Mrs. Bobbsey spoke up. She was a slender, pretty woman. She looked worried. "We've just heard that Uncle Ross is very ill," she told the children. "He has no one but us, so Daddy and I must fly to see him at once."

Mr. Bobbsey added, "We'll take Dinah and Sam to the airport. Then your mother and I will catch our plane."

"I want all of you to help Aunt Sallie keep house," said Mrs. Bobbsey.

"Goody!" cried Flossie. "We can play house all the time!"

Nan gave the box of candy to Dinah and Sam, and all four of the twins wished the couple a happy trip.

"I made this for you," said Flossie, handing Dinah the red envelope.

The stout motherly-looking woman opened it and took out the picture Flossie had drawn of Dinah and Sam under a palm tree.

"Well, that's just beautiful!" Dinah said and hugged the little girl.

Sam beamed. "The best going-away card I ever saw!"

"If we don't leave right away," Mr. Bobbsey put in, "we'll miss our planes."

Flossie threw her arms around her mother and after much kissing and hugging, the travelers left. As the young twins waved from the window, Aunt Sallie said, "We'll have a good time together, don't worry. Just remember I'm a teeny bit deaf and you must talk loudly."

"We know," said Nan with a smile. Mrs. Sallie Pry often stayed with the twins when their parents were away. She was not really their aunt, but they were very fond of her.

"If we laugh, Aunt Sallie," Nan said loudly, "you know we aren't laughing at *you*—but only because it's funny."

"Yes," replied Aunt Sallie, her eyes twinkling. "I do say odd things sometimes."

Nan picked up Aunt Sallie's coat from a chair and said to Flossie, "I'll hang this up. You put her hat in the closet."

Aunt Sallie looked surprised. "Oh, don't do that. The poor thing won't get any air."

For a moment the children looked puzzled, then Nan spoke up loudly. "I said *hat.*"

Aunt Sallie rolled her eyes. "There I go! I thought you said cat." She chuckled and the twins giggled.

While Bert took the suitcase up to the guest room, the girls and Freddie followed Aunt Sallie to the kitchen. A large black cat with a white streak under his chin was seated by the door washing his paws.

"Well, Snoop!" said Aunt Sallie. "I guess you want your supper." She stroked the cat's soft fur.

"I'll get it for him," said Flossie, going to the refrigerator.

A large, long-haired white dog walked in from the dining room.

"Now you have to pet Snap, Aunt Sallie," Flossie said.

"Set the trap?" asked the woman. "Why?"

"SNAP!" Flossie cried loudly.

"Oh my, yes, of course!" exclaimed Aunt Sallie, seeing the dog. "My old friend, Snap!" She patted his head.

That evening after supper Bert took Freddie aside and told him about the Valentine present for Flossie. Nan whispered to Flossie there was one for Freddie. When the young twins went to bed, each fell asleep wondering what wonderful surprise was to be given to the other.

The next morning when Flossie woke up, she saw her sister standing at the window in her robe and slippers.

"Come see what happened last night!" Nan said, her eyes sparkling.

Flossie ran over and looked out. "It snowed!" she exclaimed. "Oh, isn't it bee-yoo-ti-ful!"

After school that afternoon the older boys began throwing snowballs at one another and at telephone poles and brick walls. When Bert and his friend Charlie Mason passed the Springer house, Bert said, "Let's try hitting that iron deer near the house."

"Sure thing. You fire first."

Bert missed. Charlie took a turn. He missed.

Danny Rugg and Jack Westley had been watching. They began to laugh uproariously.

"You guys couldn't hit a target if your snowball was on a wire running right to that deer's head," Danny said. "You know why? 'Cause you're chicken! You can't aim right with gloves on."

"Oh yes?" Bert said. "How about you and I throwing at the same time and seeing who comes closest?"

"Okay. But I'll win."

Danny turned his back, leaned down to get a fistful of snow and quickly made a well-packed snowball. Charlie handed Bert one he was holding.

"I'll tell you when to start," Charlie said. "Ready? On your mark! *Throw!*"

Bert and Danny drew back their arms and let fly. Both snowballs went straight to the target. There was a plop and a metallic sound as the snow hit the deer.

A second later Jack cried out, "Oh!"

Both snowballs had hit the iron statue on one ear. It broke and dropped off!

The ear suddenly dropped off!

Instantly Danny said, "You did it, Bert. It's your fault." He and Jack scooted off as fast as they could go.

Bert turned to Charlie. "I guess both of us are to blame. But I can't see how snow could break iron. Let's go and take a look."

But the boys could not do this. The same savage dog they had seen the day before bounded toward them and would not let Bert and Charlie enter the yard.

"Okay, old fellow," said Bert. "I'll tell my dad about the accident when he comes home, and he can get in touch with Mr. Springer."

The two boys walked off, the big dog still barking furiously.

"That was a shame," Charlie remarked. "I wonder how much it'll cost to repair the deer."

"Plenty, probably. And I'll bet Danny won't pay a nickel of it."

Bert and Charlie headed for the hill where there was coasting. In the meantime Freddie had gone home to get his sled. When he walked up the front steps, the little boy saw a large box wrapped in brown paper. The name BOBBSEY was printed on it.

"Oh boy!" Freddie exclaimed. "I'll bet that's Flossie's Valentine surprise. I'd better hide it before she gets here."

He was about to ring the bell when he remembered that Aunt Sallie would not hear it. He lifted the Welcome mat, took a key from under it, and let himself in.

After leaving his boots on a rubber tray beside the door, he carried the box upstairs. He hid it in his mother's closet, then went down to the kitchen and loudly told Aunt Sallie he was going coasting.

"That's nice," she said, giving him two freshly baked molasses cookies. "Flossie said to tell you she went to Susie Larker's."

Freddie thanked her, then said, "Well, I'll go get my sled."

"Have a good time," the kindly woman said.

Snap followed Freddie as he hurried toward the wooded park some blocks from the house.

The air was ringing with shouts when he reached the coasting hill. Children in brightly colored snow clothes were whizzing down the steep track which curved near the foot of the slope.

Freddie met his twin. She was carrying Hildy, her red-haired rag doll. Flossie had left her at Susie's the day before.

"'I'm going to give Hildy a ride," she announced, and Freddie grinned.

When he saw Nan and Bert he told them about hiding the present. "Flossie'll never find it," he said.

Nan lay down on her sled and went speeding along the crowded hill. Suddenly a sled with two girls on it veered toward her. As they yelled, Nan swerved and shot off the track. She headed straight for a thick hedge at the bottom!

Nan could not stop. *Wham* she went, right through the hedge. Her sled bumped to a stop, and Nan looked up. For a moment she could not believe what she saw just ahead of her.

"A fairy-tale house!" she exclaimed.

CHAPTER III

THE MYSTERIOUS PLAY HOUSE

THE little house was one story high and had a peaked roof. There was a tiny window over the front door, and one on each side of it. A little arched wooden bridge led over the frozen creek in front and swirling snow made ghost-like dancing figures around the house.

"It's really a play house," Nan thought. "But how darling! Covered with snow, it certainly looks like a fairy-tale house."

"Nan, are you okay?" came Bert's voice.

She turned to see her twin crawling through the hole her sled had made in the hedge.

"Look what I found!" she cried.

As Nan pointed to the play house, Freddie, Flossie, and Susie came through the hedge. Snap followed, barking excitedly and licking Nan's face.

"How bee-yoo-ti-ful!" cried Flossie, who was still clutching Hildy.

"I wonder who owns it," said Bert. "There's no main house around here."

"Let's look in the windows," Freddie suggested.

Nan hurried across the bridge first. The others ran after her. They peered into the two frosty downstairs windows.

"I can't see anything," Freddie complained.

"Breathe on the glass," said Nan. "That'll melt the ice." The children panted hard against the panes.

"I see!" cried Flossie. "It's the living room!"

"Oooh, a little table and chairs," said Susie. "Aren't they darling?"

"Look up in this tree," said Freddie. He pointed to a platform among the snowy branches of a maple by the house.

"That's cool!" Bert exclaimed. "I'll bet some kids had a lookout post up there."

The older twins and Freddie circled the house. They saw a small shiny metal tank standing against the back wall.

"It's bottled gas for a stove," Bert remarked.

When they came around to the front of the house, Flossie was holding Hildy up to look in the window.

"I wish we could go inside!" said Susie.

Just then Snap barked loudly. The children turned to see a thin man in a brown woolen cap and coat come through the hedge.

"What are you doing here?" he asked, but he was not cross. "This is private property."

"We're sorry," said Nan, and explained what had happened.

"Whose play house is this?" Flossie asked.

"It belonged to the Springer children," the man replied.

"Springer!" Bert exclaimed. "Is this the back of that estate?"

"Yes." The man pointed up the hill behind the play house. They could see a gray roof just over the rise. "There's the mansion. I'm Henry Thurbell, the caretaker. Mr. Springer rented the property to Mr. John Harden of Florida. He hasn't moved up yet, but everything's ready for him. Today I had the telephone connected."

"You look familiar to me, Mr. Thurbell," said Bert.

"I do odd jobs for Mr. Tetlow. You've seen me in his yard, I guess."

Nan introduced all the children.

"Did you see the broken deer?" Bert asked.

"Yes. Did you do that?"

"I don't know. Another boy and I threw snowballs, and both of them hit the ear. I was going to ask my dad to find Mr. Springer and tell him. Dad's away for a few days."

"I see," said Thurbell. "I'll tell Mr. Springer. Who was the other boy?"

"Danny Rugg."

Nan spoke up. "When is the new owner going to move in?"

"I don't know. I've never seen him. He got in touch with me by mail."

At this moment they heard the deep-throated barking of a dog in the distance. Snap began yipping.

"There goes that dog again," the caretaker said. "Mr. Harden ordered me to buy a watchdog. He said to get a fierce one to keep busybodies out, but I'm afraid this one is too wild. He keeps breaking his rope and running loose."

"I think he's the one who jumped on Flossie," said Bert. "Is he a big brown German Shepherd?"

"Yes. That sounds like Rex."

"It happened yesterday," Nan put in. "I guess you saw us from the bedroom window."

Mr. Thurbell shook his head. "No. I was out all afternoon."

"But I'm sure somebody was looking out of an upstairs window," said Nan.

"What! Are you sure?"

"Yes."

Mr. Thurbell shook his head. "I can't understand it. No one but myself has a key."

Meanwhile Flossie and Susie had been peering through the play house windows.

"I wish we could go inside," Flossie said to the caretaker. "Would you let us?"

Mr. Thurbell looked at the little girl's eager face. "You promise to be very careful and not break anything?"

"Oh, yes."

"All right, then," he said. "The door is unlocked. Mr. Harden sent me keys for everything else except the play house. I found it open." He walked off toward the mansion.

Flossie opened the small front door and led the way inside. Faded yellow curtains hung at the windows and a worn flowered rug covered the floor. The children went through an arch into the back room, which was a kitchen.

"Oh, a little stove!" cooed Flossie.

"Does it work?" Freddie asked.

"I think so," said Bert, examining it. "Here are some metal tubes in the back. They must connect to the gas tank we saw."

"Then you can really cook on it," said Susie. "There's a little kettle."

Bert said, puzzled, "It's funny! Everything here is old-fashioned and faded, but the gas tank outside looks shiny and new."

"You mean," Nan asked, "that somebody might be using the stove?"

"Could be."

Nan walked over to a wooden ladder that led up through a hole in the ceiling.

"Let's explore the attic," she said, starting to climb.

The boys followed her. They found themselves on a platform under the roof. Straight ahead was a door with a padlock on it.

"I wonder what's in there," Freddie said.

Bert shrugged, but looked puzzled. "The padlock is brand new, too."

"It's odd that someone bothered to lock the attic closet but not the play house," said Nan.

"It's the play house's mystery," Freddie added, as the children filed down to the kitchen.

Flossie and Susie were looking in the dish cupboard. Hildy had been placed in an old-fashioned rocker by the table.

Suddenly loud barking and snarling came from the yard.

"It sounds like a fight!" Bert exclaimed.

The children ran outside. Snap and the big brown dog were growling and biting at each other.

"Stop it!" cried Bert.

He scooped up handfuls of snow and threw it on the dogs. Quickly Freddie and the girls did the same. Finally the big shepherd broke away from Snap.

"Go away!" shouted Bert, chasing him off.

"Poor Snap's paw is hurt," said Nan as her twin came running back. The dog was whining and holding up his right front leg.

Bert examined it gently. "We'd better take him to the vet."

"Stop it!" cried Bert

"We'll have to pull him on a sled," said Flossie.

Snap was placed on Nan's sled. The other children went for theirs, then they all started off. Bert pulled the dog.

In a little while they reached a small red brick building in the shopping district. Bert and Nan lifted Snap off the sled. Freddie rang the bell and opened the door for them to carry the dog inside.

The waiting room was empty. In a few moments an inner door opened, and a young man wearing a white coat and horn-rimmed glasses came out.

"Hello, Dr. Kern," said Nan. It was not the first time one of the Bobbsey pets had been brought to his office.

Quickly Nan explained what had happened. Dr. Kern carried Snap into his office. All the children followed and watched silently as he put the dog on a table and examined the paw.

"Don't worry," Dr. Kern said. "I'll fix him up good as new, but you'll have to leave him here for a few days."

The children heaved sighs of relief. After thanking the doctor, they said good-by to Snap and left.

Outside, Flossie suddenly exclaimed, "I forgot Hildy! She's still in the play house!"

"We'll stop and get her," said Nan.

When the children reached the Springer mansion, she suggested they take a shortcut to the play house.

Freddie spoke up, "You don't need Bert and me. Why don't we go home?"

Bert agreed, and the two boys went up the street. When the girls reached the slope that led down to the play house, Flossie said, "Nan, you don't have to come. Susie and I'll get Hildy."

"All right. I'll wait here."

The two little girls hurried down the snowy slope. By now the winter sunlight was fading. At the bottom of the hill, the play house stood in deep shadow under the big tree.

"It's kind of spooky," Susie whispered.

Flossie opened the door and started inside, then stopped short. From upstairs came a long, hollow moan!

CHAPTER IV

THE HIDDEN PACKAGE

THE two little girls stood still for a moment. Then they ran screaming from the play house and dashed up the hill to Nan.

"A spook!" Susie gasped.

"Upstairs in the play house!" Flossie added. "He made a terrible sound."

"What kind of a sound?" Nan asked. "Maybe it was the wind."

"No, it wasn't," Flossie insisted. "It sounded like this." She gave a long, low, howling moan. Susie joined in. Nan decided the girls really had heard something more than the wind.

"I didn't get Hildy," Flossie sobbed. "Nan, will you go back with us?"

"It's getting dark," her sister said. "I'm afraid Aunt Sallie will worry if we don't show up soon."

"All right," Flossie agreed. "But I hope the spook won't hurt Hildy."

"Listen, Flossie," said Nan, putting an arm around her little sister, "you know there are no such things as spooks."

"I—I guess not," Flossie agreed.

At dinner that evening Flossie told what had happened at the play house.

"Somebody must have been playing a trick on you," said Bert. "Maybe Danny Rugg."

Nan was thinking. "No. I believe it's part of the mystery at the place—the face at the Springer window, the new padlock on the attic door in the play house, and the new gas tank. I wonder if somebody is staying in the play house without Mr. Thurbell knowing it."

Aunt Sallie had not heard much of what was being said. She had been busy serving the children. Suddenly she put down her fork and looked at Freddie.

"Oh dear!" she exclaimed. "I meant to tell you! How could I have forgotten!"

"What did you forget?" asked Freddie, surprised.

"The fire engine for you."

The little boy's eyes grew big. He loved fire engines and hoped to be a fireman when he grew up.

"For me?" he said happily. "Where is it?"

"You'll get the toy tomorrow," Aunt Sallie said. "It's a very old one. I found it in my basement when I was cleaning. One of the wheels was broken off, so I took it to the toy hospital."

"Oh boy! Thanks!" said Freddie loudly.

"You can pick it up after school," said Aunt Sallie, smiling. "It's paid for."

When dinner was over, the children carried their plates to the kitchen.

"We'll help you wash the dishes, Aunt Sallie," said Flossie.

Aunt Sallie looked surprised as she closed the refrigerator door. "Fishes! What fishes?"

"Dishes!" all the children said together.

Aunt Sallie chuckled. "That makes more sense than washing fishes!"

All this time Nan had been getting ready to wrap some left-over chocolate cake in waxed paper. Suddenly the paper rose into the air and fluttered over the kitchen table.

"The paper's floating!" Freddie exclaimed. Everyone burst into laughter.

A second later it drifted to the floor.

Bert said, "I felt a cold draft. That could have blown it. Maybe the front door blew open."

But when he checked, Bert found that it was closed. So were the windows.

"That's strange," he thought, and reported what he had seen.

"Maybe somebody opened the door," said Freddie, "and came in."

Everyone hunted for a possible intruder but

"The paper's floating!" Freddie exclaimed

could find nothing wrong. The flying paper remained a mystery.

After the kitchen was tidied, the twins did their homework, then went to watch television with Aunt Sallie. A short time afterward, the doorbell rang. Nan hurried to answer.

"Nellie Parks!" she cried, hugging her best friend.

"Hi!" Nellie said cheerily, holding up a paper sack. "Would you like some rainbow corn? Daddy brought it home tonight. Besides, I have a wonderful idea to tell you."

"I have news for you, too," said Nan.

Nellie took off her hooded coat and shook out her dark blond hair. Her pretty face was pink with cold. Nan led the way into the living room where the others were watching television.

"Hello, Mrs. Pry," said Nellie loudly.

Aunt Sallie knew all the Bobbseys' friends, and she smiled at the visitor. "Glad to see you again, my dear," she said.

"May we pop some corn?" Nan asked.

"Of course. If the tops are torn, I'll sew them."

The twins grinned. "Popcorn!" they said loudly.

Aunt Sallie struck her forehead with one hand. "My goodness, yes!"

The children trooped to the kitchen. Soon the butter was sizzling in the pan and the corn was dancing and exploding in the big electric popper.

"Now tell us your idea, Nellie," said Nan.

"A Valentine party! Wouldn't it be fun?"

"Oh, yes!" Nan exclaimed, and Flossie clapped her hands excitedly.

Freddie's eyes sparkled. "We can have lots of ice cream and candy and cake—"

Bert had not said anything. "Don't you like the idea?" Nellie asked him.

"It's okay," he said. "But fellows don't like all that Valentine mush. It'll be okay if you have some cool games and plenty to eat."

Nan grinned. "We'll see that you get lots of food. Maybe we could have the party here. The younger kids can be in the basement and we'll be up here."

"We'll shop for supplies tomorrow," said Nellie eagerly.

The telephone rang and Flossie ran to answer it. A moment later they heard her shriek. "It's Mommy! Come quick, everybody!"

Nan greeted her mother excitedly. "How is Uncle Ross?" she asked.

"No better, I'm afraid," Mrs. Bobbsey said. "I don't know how long we'll have to stay. How's everybody at home?"

"Fine," Nan assured her. "Mother, may we have a Valentine party here?"

"Yes, if Aunt Sallie doesn't mind."

After each twin had talked to both parents and told them about the play house mystery, Aunt Sallie spoke with Mrs. Bobbsey. The children started for the kitchen.

Bert snapped his fingers. "I forgot to tell Mother and Dad about the broken deer."

Nan replied, "It's just as well. They have enough to worry about."

The twins walked into the kitchen just as Nellie put a big bowl of multi-colored popcorn on the table.

"It's bee-yoo-ti-ful!" exclaimed Flossie.

"You can see why it's called rainbow corn," said Nellie. "Help yourselves."

"Umm, good," said Bert, munching a handful.

Nan filled a small wooden bowl with popcorn and took it to Aunt Sallie. When she came back, they talked over plans for the party.

"Maybe I can wear my new red dress," said Flossie. "Would you like to see it, Nellie? I'll show it to you."

She ran up the stairs two at a time and hurried into her parents' bedroom. She clicked on the light, then opened her mother's closet. The dress was hanging there, waiting for Mrs. Bobbsey to shorten it. Suddenly Flossie saw the large box wrapped in brown paper.

"I'll bet that's Freddie's Valentine surprise!" she thought. "I didn't know it came!" She guessed Nan and Bert must have put it in the closet. "If Freddie looks in here he'll see it right away. I'll hide it better."

Flossie decided to put the box in the linen closet next to the attic door. She picked up the awkward package and went down to the end of the hall. The hinges on the door squeaked as she opened it. Flossie laid the box on the floor behind a portable sewing machine.

"Freddie'll never find the surprise here!" she thought.

At that moment a board overhead creaked. Flossie's heart gave a little thump. Quickly she shut the door and hurried back to the bedroom. She grabbed her dress, flicked the wall switch, and ran downstairs.

"Here it is. Do you like it?" she asked Nellie.

"It's darling."

As Nellie took the dress, Flossie pulled Nan's sleeve. She made wild signs with her fingers, trying to explain about the box. But the little girl stopped as she caught Freddie staring at her.

"What are you doing?" he asked.

"Nothing," his twin replied. "It's just sort of a game."

A few minutes later she managed to whisper in Nan's ear without anyone noticing. Nan smiled and nodded. The joke was working well!

After the young twins had gone to bed, Nan

told Nellie about the mystery on the Springer estate.

"It sounds scary," her friend said.

In a few minutes Nellie's father came to take her home, then Nan went to bed.

A little later Flossie awoke. She was very thirsty. "I'll go get a drink," she decided.

As Flossie sat up in bed she heard a loud *squee-eek.*

"The linen closet door!" the little girl thought. "I'll bet Freddie's hunting for the Valentine surprise. He can't have it yet!"

Flossie found her slippers and opened the door. She looked down the long, darkened hallway but could see no one. But she was sure her twin was moving the box from its hiding place.

"Freddie Bobbsey," she called softly, "you put that back!"

There was no answer.

CHAPTER V

STOLEN TOYS

"FREDDIE!" his twin called again. Still no answer.

Flossie hurried back inside her room and shook Nan, who was asleep.

"What's the matter?" Nan asked sleepily.

"Freddie's peeking at his surprise. I heard the door hinges squeak."

Nan sighed, got up, and put on her robe and slippers. The two girls left the room, and Nan switched on the bright light in the hall. No one was there.

"We'd better check the box," Flossie whispered.

Quietly the sisters went down to the linen closet. The door was partly open.

"I closed it. I know I did," Flossie said. She felt behind the sewing machine. "The package is still here."

"Freddie probably scooted back to bed as soon as you came to get me," Nan suggested.

"But he knows where the surprise is," Flossie whispered. "We'd better move it to my closet."

Nan took the box from its hiding place and the girls started back. On the way they stopped to peer into the boys' room. Freddie was curled up under the covers, apparently sound asleep.

"He might be playing possum," Nan said. "Come on, Floss, let's go back to bed."

In the morning Nan called her little brother aside. "What were you doing at the linen closet last night?" she asked.

Freddie looked at her in amazement. "What do you mean?"

"Flossie heard the hinges squeak," Nan said, "and you left the door open."

"I don't know what you're talking about, honest."

Freddie looked so puzzled that Nan believed him. "Maybe Flossie dreamed the whole thing," she said.

"What's all the mystery about?" Freddie asked curiously.

"I wonder too," his sister replied and walked off.

After breakfast, while the young twins were getting into their snow jackets and boots, Nan beckoned Bert into the kitchen with Aunt Sallie. She closed the door, then asked loudly if either of them had looked in the linen closet during the night. Both said no.

Nan told them what Flossie had heard.

Aunt Sallie's eyes grew wide. "Maybe we had a burglar!" she exclaimed.

"We'd better see if anything is missing," Bert suggested.

"All right, but hurry or you'll be late for school," said Aunt Sallie.

Quickly she checked the family silver, while the older twins went through all the rooms. Nothing was out of place. Every door and window was locked. The whole thing was still a puzzle.

Aunt Sallie remarked, "You children seem to be getting into all sorts of mysteries. Do be careful."

Bert and Nan left the house together. Nan met Nellie and walked with her while Bert ran on ahead. When he reached the Springer mansion, Bert saw Danny Rugg and Jack Westley scuffling through the snow in the front yard.

"Looking for something?" Bert called.

The two boys turned. Seeing Bert, Danny burst out, "Yes, you. I want my ring back!"

Bert stared at the bully. "Your ring? For Pete's sake what are you talking about?"

"Huh! You know all right. I lost it here the other day. Jack and I left before you did."

"So what?"

"So you found it, Bert Bobbsey, and took it!"

"Oh, go get lost," said Bert. "I don't know anything about your old ring. What does it look like?"

"It's silver color and has a funny face on top." Danny hesitated. "It's a trick ring. When you press a spring, the top flies up. My initials are scratched inside. But you know this, Bert. You give it back or I'll—" The bully doubled up his fists.

"So you want to fight?" Bert said. "Okay."

Danny sneered. "How'd you like to take a bloody nose to school?" He laughed.

Bert advanced toward the bully. "Nobody's going to call me a thief!"

Jack grabbed his pal's arm. "Danny, don't fight! You know what happened to you last time you—"

"Oh, okay," Danny said. "But I'm telling you, Bert Bobbsey, if you don't give that ring back to me, you'll be sorry."

Bert walked off but called back, "I'll try to find it for you. And by the way you'll have to pay half the bill for mending that deer."

"Oh yeah?" said Danny. "Try and make me."

After school Bert asked Charlie to help him hunt for Danny's ring in the snow on the front lawn of the Springer home. "I guess Danny thinks it fell off when he was throwing snowballs!"

The boys went off just as Nan and Flossie met. "You promised to go with me and get Hildy," the little girl reminded her sister.

"We'll go right now," Nan said, and started off with Flossie.

They reached the slope leading to the play house and trooped down the hill.

"The front door is closed," Flossie whispered. "Susie and I left it open when we ran away."

"Maybe Mr. Thurbell shut it," said Nan.

Nan knocked on the door. There was no answer, so she and her sister walked into the little house. Flossie rushed over to get her doll.

The rocking chair was empty!

"My dolly's been stolen! Hildy's gone!" she cried.

"Are you sure this is where you left her?" Nan asked.

"Course I am! I put her right here!" Flossie pointed a chubby finger at the chair.

The two girls searched the small play house, but could not find the rag doll. Flossie was on the verge of tears.

"Maybe Mr. Thurbell found Hildy and took her away," Nan suggested. "Let's go over and ask him."

She and Flossie left the house and shut the door. They climbed the hill to the mansion and rang the back doorbell.

After a few moments the caretaker appeared.

He was wearing an old gray sweater and pants. His brown hair was neatly combed.

"Hello, girls," he said. "What can I do for you?"

Quickly Nan told him about the missing doll, and Flossie asked, "Did you take Hildy, Mr. Thurbell?"

The caretaker shook his head. "No, I haven't seen her."

Flossie told him about the moan she and Susie had heard the day before.

"Hmm," the caretaker remarked. "I'll have to look into this."

"Who could it be?" Nan asked, puzzled.

"I don't know," he replied.

Nan asked him about the new padlock and gas tank at the play house.

Mr. Thurbell shrugged. "Mr. Springer had a part-time watchman who checked over the place just before I came. I guess he thought it best to lock the attic closet and leave the stove ready for use." Then the caretaker turned to Flossie. "I make the rounds of the property every day, and I'll keep an eye out for your dolly."

"Somebody stole her!" Flossie wailed.

Nan thanked Mr. Thurbell and turned to leave. As they went down the porch steps, she saw that her sister's chin was trembling.

"The spook kidnapped Hildy," said Flossie.

Nan put her arm around the little girl.

"My dolly's been stolen!" Flossie cried

"Cheer up. We'll find her. Meantime, we'd better buy our Valentine supplies."

On the way through Lakeport Nan stopped at the Goody Shoppe and bought a bag of cinnamon hearts to cheer up Flossie. Freddie was just passing by.

"I'm going to pick up my fire engine," he told them.

"We'll be in the five-and-ten, Freddie," Nan said, "shopping for the Valentine party."

The little boy nodded and ran down the street to the Kundy Toy Shop. Just then a car drew up to the curb. The driver, wearing a gray overcoat and a green muffler, got out. He was of medium height.

Freddie entered the store. A young man with curly blond hair stood behind the counter. He knew the Bobbseys. "I know what you came for," he said, smiling.

Freddie's eyes sparkled. "Is it ready, Mr. Kundy?"

"Yes."

As he hurried to the rear of the shop, Freddie glanced out the window. The stranger in the gray coat was looking in.

A few minutes later Mr. Kundy came back, carrying a bright red metal fire engine. It had a gold-colored bell on top and large wheels. Four horses were pulling it.

"Oh, it's cool!" Freddie exclaimed. He took

the toy in both hands and rang the little bell.

"Take it easy," Mr. Kundy warned. "That's a valuable antique. You can't bang it around the way you do your other fire engines."

"I'll be careful," said Freddie.

He thanked Mr. Kundy and left the shop. The man in the gray overcoat was still looking in the window.

"That's a great engine you have there, young fellow," he said as the boy came out. He smiled, showing big white teeth, but dark glasses hid his eyes.

"Yes, it's an antique," said Freddie proudly.

"I'm a fire engine buff," the man told him.

"A what?" the little boy asked politely.

"Buff," the man repeated. "That means they're my hobby."

"They're mine too," said Freddie.

"May I have a look at your engine?" the man asked.

"Sure, but be careful of it," Freddie replied.

He handed over the toy. As the man stared at it, he slid one hand into his pocket. He brought it out again closed.

"Listen," he said earnestly, "will you do me a favor?"

Freddie looked surprised. "What is it?"

"Put out your hand."

Freddie did as he was asked. "Just hold this for a minute," the stranger said. He placed something in Freddie's palm. The boy looked down.

"It's a dollar bill!" he exclaimed.

As he looked up, the man went striding toward the car at the curb. "Stop!" cried Freddie, hurrying after him, "I don't want this! Give me my engine!"

"Thanks for selling it," the man called with a grin and swung into the car.

"Wait! I didn't sell it!" Freddie exclaimed.

But the man had slammed the door. As Freddie pulled on the handle, the stranger started the car and it shot forward.

Freddie was yanked off his feet and fell in the street!

CHAPTER VI

THE MEAN MAN

FREDDIE jumped up unhurt. "Come back!" he cried and ran after the car. But it disappeared around the next corner.

Biting his lip to keep from crying, the little boy raced down the street to the five-and-ten. His sisters were just coming out, carrying several parcels.

"It's—it's gone!" Freddie told them. "My fire engine!"

"What happened?" Nan asked quickly.

He told his story.

"That's terrible," said Nan. She saw the dollar still in her brother's hand. "The engine was worth much more than that. The man wasn't *exactly* stealing, but he was very close to it."

"We ought to tell the policeman," said Flossie indignantly.

"We will," Nan declared firmly. "We'll go to headquarters right now."

In a little while the three children were ushered into Chief Smith's office. He smiled at them. "Well, how are my favorite detectives?" he asked. The Bobbsey twins had worked with the police a number of times on their little mysteries.

Freddie told what had happened and described the thief.

"I believe we are already looking for this same fellow," he said. "Several reports have come from people in the Lakeport area who have sold a man their antique toys for very little money. Later they learned the toys were valuable. The man pretends they are junk and offers to take them off the person's hands."

"Do you know who he is?" Nan asked.

The chief shook his head. "No. He used a different name every time."

Flossie spoke up. "His name should be Mr. Mean."

The chief agreed, and thanked the children for reporting to him. They went home feeling sad.

A few minutes later Bert came in. Aunt Sallie served supper at once. While they ate, Freddie told what had happened to the fire engine and described the man.

Bert was angry. "The nerve of him! We'll try to get your engine back again, Freddie. What did it look like?"

Freddie described the thief

Freddie described the toy.

"Hildy's missing too," Flossie spoke up and told about going to the play house for the doll.

"Lots of things are missing," Bert said. "Danny Rugg's ring is gone. He says I took it. Charlie and I hunted in the snow for an hour, but we couldn't find it."

The children had talked loudly enough for Mrs. Pry to hear them. "Dear, dear," she said. "What a lot of trouble you're having."

"We sure are," Freddie said, sighing.

Next morning was Saturday. After the twins had helped Aunt Sally with the breakfast dishes and made their own beds, Nan called the veterinarian to find out how Snap was. The others stood around the telephone and listened. Finally she put down the receiver.

"May we bring him home today?" Flossie asked.

"No. He has to stay there for a few more days," Nan replied.

Flossie sighed. "I miss him and I guess he's lonesome for us, too. And Snoop's too big to play with."

"Why don't you go over to Susie's house and play with her kittens?" Nan suggested.

Flossie agreed and Freddie decided to go coasting with Bert. Nan went to Nellie's house to make Valentine favors.

A little while before noon Flossie came home,

hungry for lunch. She took the key from under the mat, unlocked the front door, and stepped inside. She stopped short with a gasp.

A strange man was tiptoeing up the stairs!

"Oh!" Flossie exclaimed. "What do you want?"

With a choking cry, the man whirled. He bolted down the stairs, pushed Flossie aside, then ran out and leaped off the porch. He hurried to a car at the curb and drove off.

"Aunt Sallie!" Flossie cried, running to the kitchen. "There was a strange man in here!"

Mrs. Pry turned, surprised. "What's the matter? What pan?"

"No, no, not a pan—a man!" Flossie shouted. Talking loudly, she managed to make Aunt Sallie understand what had happened.

Just then Bert's and Freddie's voices sounded from the hall. Flossie and Aunt Sallie hurried to meet them, just as Nan arrived. She came inside and closed the door. Flossie excitedly told her story.

"How could the man have gotten in?" asked Aunt Sallie, shaking her head.

"Maybe he knew the key was under the mat," Freddie burst out.

"I think we should change its hiding place," said Nan.

Bert quickly opened the door and took the key from the lock where Flossie had left it. "Better still, I'll have four more of these made by the locksmith, and each of us can carry one."

Aunt Sallie heard him and said she already had a key which his mother had given her. "But I'll have three more made when I go to the store today," she added.

"We must tell the police about this," Bert said. "I guess the fellow was a sneak thief." He telephoned headquarters.

The girls helped Aunt Sallie put lunch on the table. As they ate soup and sandwiches, Bert questioned Flossie. "What did the fellow look like?"

"He was—about medium tall. I didn't see his face much. But I remember he had on a gray hat and coat and a green muffler around his neck."

"Maybe it's Mr. Mean!" said Freddie. *"He* looked like that."

A police officer arrived and heard the story. "The fellow you call Mr. Mean seems to be interested only in antique toys. Do you have any?"

"Not that we know of," Nan replied.

After the officer had left, Nan called her twin aside. "I've been thinking—maybe the gingerbread house is an antique, even though Mrs. Villey didn't say so."

"If it is," said Bert, "the man Flossie saw really might have been Mr. Mean. And if he used the key to get in here today, he could have come in with it night before last. But how did he learn we have the toy?"

"Say, he could be the same man who was at Mrs. Villey's when we bought the gingerbread house for Freddie and Flossie," Nan exclaimed.

Bert agreed. "And if he did sneak in here that night, it explains why the paper blew off the table and why Flossie heard the closet door squeak."

Nan made a little face. "It's creepy to think he must have been in the house all that time."

The doorbell rang. Bert answered. Charlie Mason stood there.

"Some of us are going skating," he said. "How about coming along?"

"Okay. I'll get my coat and skates."

"I want to go!" cried Freddie, running into the hall with Flossie.

"Okay. Why don't you all come? But hurry up," said Charlie.

On the way to the pond they picked up Ralph Blake, a friend of Bert's. Freddie's pal, freckle-nosed Teddy Blake, joined them, and also Susie Larker.

As they came to the shore of the pond, they saw a large bonfire. Nellie Parks's father was there helping some of the older boys build up the blaze.

"Look who's here!" Freddie said to Flossie. Standing at the edge of the woods were Danny and Jack.

At once Flossie ran up to them. "I want to ask you a question, Danny," she said. "Did you take my doll Hildy?"

Bert's friends burst into laughter, and several other boys came over. One said in a little-girl voice, "Pwease come'n pway house with me."

Danny grew red.

Flossie went on, "If you did take it, I want it back!"

"I didn't take any doll!" Danny declared angrily.

"Sorry," said Flossie. She turned away and started to put on her skates.

In a few minutes the Bobbseys and their friends were skimming over the ice.

"Let's have a race!" cried Bert.

There were shouts of approval as six boys besides Bert lined up. Danny and Jack did not join in. They skated out on the pond and stood still to watch the race. Danny was fooling around with a hockey stick.

"On your mark!" Bert shouted. "Get set! Go!"

The racers sped off. Bert soon edged out ahead of the others. A moment later Danny swooped past the boys and flung his hockey stick in front of Bert, who tried to pull aside.

But he stumbled on the stick and fell sprawling into the path of the racers. Yelling, three of them crashed down on top of him.

There was a sudden *crack!* The ice was breaking!

CHAPTER VII

THE SNOW GHOST

"GET off!" cried Bert in a muffled voice. "Quick! The ice is cracking!"

Swiftly the boys who had piled on top of Bert rolled off him. Before he could move, someone grabbed his legs and dragged him backward.

"That's far enough," came Charlie's voice. "We're safe here!"

"Are you hurt?" Ralph asked as Bert got to his knees.

"I'm okay," he said, catching his breath. "How about the rest of you?"

"We're all right," replied one of the skaters. "Lucky we didn't go through the ice." He pointed to the cracks which spread out from the spot where the four boys had hit. Getting to his feet, Bert picked up Danny's hockey stick.

Charlie said angrily, "Let's teach those two guys a lesson!"

Some distance away the two bullies were skating slowly in a circle watching the racers and grinning.

"Okay, Danny! We'll get you for this!" shouted Charlie.

Yelling, the seven boys struck off across the ice. Instantly Danny and Jack skated fast for the shore.

"Cut them off!" shouted Bert.

The racers swerved and bore down on the fleeing bullies. Reaching the snowy embankment, Danny and Jack floundered into the woods without stopping to take off their skates. Their pursuers followed. Before they had gone ten steps, Bert dropped the hockey stick and tackled Danny while Charlie brought down Jack.

"Stop it! Help!" yelled the bullies, while the boys washed their faces in snow and put some down their backs.

"That's enough!" said Bert.

The seven racers took the few steps back to the lake and skated off to where the bonfire was. After removing their skates, they walked over to Nan and Nellie, who were opening a large box.

"Nellie's father brought lots of marshmallows for everybody," said Nan.

Freddie, Flossie, and several other children came from the woods where they had been picking up long sticks.

"We'll roast the marshmallows on these," said Flossie.

In a little while all the skaters except Danny and Jack had gathered around the fire and were toasting marshmallows. As they ate the hot sticky sweets, Mr. Parks put more wood on the fire. The afternoon sun had disappeared and the trees seemed to grow taller and darker around them.

"Who knows a ghost story?" Nellie asked.

"I do," said Charlie. "Did you ever hear about the snow ghost?"

There was a chorus of no's and somebody called, "Tell us."

Charlie looked very serious and began in a low voice. "This story was told by an old Indian who escaped from the snow ghost. He said that one winter he and his friend were lost in the North Woods during a bad storm. It was dark and the wind was blowing. Suddenly they heard a terrible screech and saw a swirling white thing among the trees. It swooped around them howling. It spun them round and round and swept his friend away. He never came back!"

"What happened to him?" Flossie asked, big-eyed.

"No one would ever have known," Charlie replied soberly, "but the Indian ran after his friend. He saw him fall through a big black hole in the snow, way down into the earth!"

"That's scary," said Freddie.

"Is it a real story, or did you make it all up?" Nan asked.

Charlie grinned. "That's for me to know and you to find out."

"Very funny!" called a sour voice.

The children at the fire looked up to see Danny and Jack standing near the edge of the woods with their skates slung over their shoulders.

"Pay no attention to them," said Nan in a disgusted voice.

"I think it's going to snow again," remarked Mr. Parks, looking up at the sky. "It's getting pretty dark. Take one more spin, Nellie, then we'd better go."

Nearly everyone decided to leave. Some of the children helped Mr. Parks put out the bonfire while others took a last turn on the ice. As Freddie went to put on his skates, Danny called him.

"What do you want?" Freddie asked as he walked over to the two bullies.

Danny stuck his hands in his jacket pocket and grinned. "We know where you hid that big box in your house."

"You remember—the one that came day before yesterday," added Jack with a wink.

The little boy looked surprised. "How did you find out about that?"

"Never mind," said Danny in a superior

voice. "We've learned a lot of things. For instance, I can tell you just where you put it."

"You can't!" said Freddie indignantly.

"It's in the cellar," said Danny.

"No, it isn't!" retorted Freddie. "I put it in my mother's closet, so there!"

At that moment a twig cracked. Freddie looked past Danny into the woods. He caught a glimpse of a green muffler.

At the same moment his sister called, "Freddie! Be quiet!" Nan hurried over, pointing into the woods. "That man—he's been listening!"

Before the words were out of her mouth the eavesdropper ran back into the woods, and Danny and Jack raced off.

"That was Mr. Mean, I'm sure!" Nan said. She grabbed Freddie's hand. "Come on! We'd better find out where he's going."

"Let's get Bert first," said Freddie. They turned to look for their brother, but he was far out on the ice with the other boys.

"There's no time to waste," said Nan grimly. "That man is getting farther away every minute. Come on!"

Nan plunged into the deep snow in the woods. Freddie floundered after her. "Try to walk in my footprints," she told him. "It'll be easier for you."

After a few moments they stopped and looked around. "There're his tracks," said Freddie. He pointed to slashes in the snow which showed where the man had run away.

"I don't see him though," said Nan quietly. "Let's go on. Maybe we can catch up."

The running tracks zigzagged back and forth, circling and crossing.

"He's trying to throw us off his trail," Nan thought. They pushed on deeper into the woods. The laughter and calls of the skaters grew fainter.

"Wait a minute!" said Freddie, gasping and red-faced. "Let's rest a minute."

As they stood quietly, large flakes of snow began to drift down.

"Maybe we ought to go back!" said Freddie, worried.

Nan looked about uneasily. "Yes, I suppose so. If we haven't caught up with him by now, I guess we won't."

"Which way *is* back?" Freddie asked anxiously.

"That's easy," his sister replied. "We'll just follow our own tracks."

While they had been talking, the snow had been coming down harder and the wind was bending the tops of the trees. The children headed back, stepping in their own tracks. But as the snow grew heavier the footprints began to vanish.

"Soon they'll be gone altogether," Nan

thought. She went as fast as she could, but the snow was deep, and Freddie's short legs were tired.

"Wait!" he pleaded. "Let's rest."

"We must hurry, or our tracks will be gone," said Nan.

Freddie looked alarmed. "Then we'll be lost."

The children pushed on as the woods grew darker and the white flakes fell faster. Suddenly the wind howled and a swirling flurry of snow rose ahead of them. An unearthly screech filled the air.

"It's the snow ghost!" cried Freddie.

Nan grabbed her brother and held him close as the whirlwind engulfed them. A moment later it was gone. The unearthly shriek came again and Nan saw two branches scraping together.

"Don't be afraid," she said to the little boy. "It was the wind in the trees that made the noise."

"Let's get out of here," said Freddie.

The children plunged on, but the tracks had disappeared. Finally Nan stopped.

"I don't know which way to go," she admitted.

"We'll be like the man in the story," Freddie said. "Nobody will ever hear of us again. Maybe we'll fall through a hole in the snow down to the middle of the earth."

"It's the snow ghost!"

"You know that was just a story," Nan said firmly. "Charlie made up the whole thing."

"Maybe, but it seemed real." Freddie shivered.

"Nonsense!" Nan said quickly. She glanced around and saw a small rise of ground a short distance away. "You wait here. I'll climb up there. Maybe I'll be able to see the lake and then we'll know which way to go."

She hurried off through the snow while Freddie watched anxiously.

"Be careful," he warned as his sister climbed to the top of the low ridge.

"Stop worrying!" she called back.

The next moment she sank out of sight!

CHAPTER VIII

A DOUBLE TRICK

"NAN!" Freddie cried. He ran through the snow and up the low rise to the place where his sister had disappeared. Then he began to laugh.

Just below was a fountain. Water from it had squirted upward against the snowbank and frozen. Nan had slid down the ice. Now she sat on top of the fountain!

"How am I ever going to get up to you?" she asked, jumping off.

"I guess you can't," said Freddie. "I'll slide down too." Then he added, "Listen!"

Shouts sounded nearby!

"It's Bert!" Freddie cried. He ran back toward the voices. "We're here!"

Moments later Bert, Charlie, and Mr. Parks appeared among the trees.

"Come quick!" Freddie cried. "We have to pull Nan up from the frozen fountain!"

"What!" Charlie asked.

They all looked over the edge. Then Mr. Parks said, "Bert and Charlie and I will form a human chain and pull Nan up."

Freddie looked sad. "I found her. I ought to be a—a link in the chain. You can bend me right around."

The others laughed, and Mr. Parks said this would not be necessary. "Freddie, you can be last in line."

They all lay down on the ground. Bert was first at the edge of the icy slope. Then came Charlie grabbing Bert's ankles. Mr. Parks followed. Slowly Bert inched his way down. Nan grabbed his wrists and he took hers.

"Up we go!" he called.

He and the others began to wriggle toward the woods. In a few moments Nan was at the top.

"Oh, thank you," she said. "I guess it would have been a long walk home from down there."

"We're glad to see you, young lady," said Mr. Parks. "Why did you run off that way?"

"We were chasing a bad man," said Freddie, "and we saw a snow ghost."

Quickly Nan explained, and Bert said, "I wonder where the fellow went."

"I don't know," his sister replied. "He zigzagged a lot."

Mr. Parks pointed toward a ridge. "A road runs just beyond that rise. The fellow might have left his car there. By now he could be back in town."

As Mr. Parks and the children headed for the lake, Freddie noticed that Nellie's father was using a compass. "You should never go into the woods without one of these," he told them. "The trees look very much alike, and it's easy to get lost."

When they reached the clearing, Flossie ran over and threw her arms around her sister and Freddie. "Don't go away again," she begged.

Soon all the children started for home. The snow was falling very hard now. On the way Nan told Flossie and Nellie about the man she had seen listening to Freddie and Danny.

All of them were worried.

"It sure looks as if that fellow's after the surprise box," Bert remarked.

"I'll bet," said Charlie, "that the man gave Danny some money to trick Freddie into telling where the box was."

"So you did find the present after all!" Flossie said to her twin.

"Sure I did! In Mother's room. But how did you know about it?"

Flossie looked puzzled. "What about the linen closet? You saw it there, didn't you?"

Freddie grinned. "Is that why Nan asked me about that closet?" he said mysteriously. As his sister nodded, he laughed. "I told you I didn't look there."

"Then who did?" Flossie asked.

The older twins exchanged glances. "Maybe the man with the green muffler," Nan admitted.

Suddenly Flossie gave a little gasp and clapped her hand over her mouth.

"What's the matter?" Nan asked.

"I heard a board creak when I moved the box into the linen closet," Flossie said. "Maybe he was in the upstairs hall with me. It was kind of dark."

"How awful!" said Nellie.

"It might have happened that way," said Bert soberly. "The man could have been on the attic steps with the door open a crack."

"That fellow," said Charlie, "must have a lot of nerve, and he must want the box pretty bad."

Bert chuckled. "We've certainly made things tough for him. It's been in three hiding places so far!"

"But wait a minute!" Freddie spoke up. "How does Flossie know about the box? It's supposed to be her surprise."

The older twins laughed and Bert said, "I guess we'll have to tell you. The box is for both of you."

"Oh, goody!" exclaimed Flossie, clapping her hands.

"What's in it?" Freddie asked excitedly.

"That part's still a secret," Nan replied with a smile.

After dropping Charlie and Nellie at their homes, the twins hurried down the street toward their own house. They could see a light in the kitchen window.

"Aunt Sallie's cooking supper," said Nan. "I hope it'll be ready soon. I'm hungry."

Bert opened the front door. After the twins had left their boots in the tray and hung up their coats, they hurried into the kitchen.

"We're home, Aunt Sallie!" Freddie called loudly. "How soon are we—"

He stopped short. The kitchen was empty. A bowl of batter stood on the table with a spoon in it. A cup of flour was spilled beside it, and the housekeeper's apron was on the floor.

"That's funny," said Nan, frowning. "I wonder where Aunt Sallie is."

"The food is in the pots," Bert reported from the stove, "but there's no flame under them."

"This is strange," said Nan. "Aunt Sallie is very neat. It's not like her to leave things this way."

"Maybe she had to go away in a hurry," said Bert. He hastened to the hall closet. "Her coat and hat are gone," he called.

The others joined him. "Maybe she left a note," said Flossie, but they could find none.

"Perhaps she went to one of the neighbors to

get something," said Nan. While the others listened, she telephoned all the Bobbseys' nearby friends. None of them had seen or heard from the housekeeper.

"I'm awfully hungry," Freddie spoke up.

"I'll heat the food," said Nan. "Maybe Aunt Sallie will be back by then."

But an hour later there was still no word from Mrs. Pry.

"Maybe she was kidnapped—like Hildy," said Flossie.

"We'd better call the police," Bert suggested, and they all went to the telephone.

Flossie shivered. "If a bad man took Aunt Sallie away, he might come back for us."

"Listen!" said Nan sharply. She pointed to the front door.

The children turned to look. *The doorknob was turning a little!*

"Stand back!" Bert whispered.

He walked over softly and opened the door. In a cold blast of wind and snow a dark figure tumbled into the hall.

"Aunt Sallie!" cried Nan.

The children ran over to help her.

"Dear me! What happened?" she asked breathlessly, as Bert closed the door.

"That's what we want to know! Are you all right?" Nan asked.

"I'm nearly frozen," said Aunt Sallie. The

"Aunt Sallie!" cried Nan

children took off her coat and hat. "I dropped my key on the porch. While I stooped over, looking for it, I had to hold onto the doorknob."

"And then Bert opened it, and you fell inside," said Freddie.

"The key's still on the porch," she said, her teeth chattering. Bert quickly found it.

Nan served hot soup and toast to Aunt Sallie. While eating, she told her story. "A man called on the telephone and said you all had been in an accident and were being sent to Mercy Hospital.

"He told me to go there at once. Of course I dropped everything and went. It's way across town so I took a bus to the hospital. I learned the story wasn't true. I tried to get a taxi home, but because of the storm there weren't any. I waited a long time for a bus."

"What a terrible trick!" Nan exclaimed.

"Why would anyone do such a mean thing?" said the housekeeper. She was still shivering.

"Maybe you'd better take a hot bath and get into bed, Aunt Sallie," Nan said. "I'll bring up your supper on a tray."

"I couldn't eat anything more," Aunt Sallie said.

"Then go to bed and don't worry about anything," Nan said. "We'll manage fine."

Gratefully Mrs. Pry agreed and said good night. Then suddenly she exclaimed, "Your keys! I almost forgot! I had them made!" She took them from her purse, handed them to Nan, Freddie, and Flossie, then went to her room.

The twins had fun getting supper and clearing it away afterward. But there were a few accidents. First Flossie spilled gravy on the kitchen floor.

"Oh dear." She sighed. "I wish Snap was here to lick this up." She grabbed a dozen paper towels to sop up the slippery mess.

Freddie laughed but got too close and *whoops!* his feet skidded, and down he went. "Ugh!" he cried, and fell several more times before he could get up.

Bert wiped the gravy from him, then said, "You'd better take off your clothes and put them in the washing machine."

The little boy scooted upstairs to undress, while Bert carried the vacuum cleaner into the dining room. A moment later Nan heard him yell.

"What's the matter?" she asked, running in.

"A mouse got sucked into the cleaner."

"A mouse!"

"Oh, not a real one—Snoop's toy mouse."

Nan giggled, then went back to the kitchen. Now it was her turn to yell. She had put too much soap powder into the dishwasher. The foam was oozing out of the machine and covering the floor.

"Anyway," she said, as the other children

rushed to her, "the suds will take care of the grease the gravy left! I'm afraid," she added, "we aren't such good housekeepers after all!"

When the young twins had gone to bed, Bert and Nan talked over the hoax played on Aunt Sallie.

"I think Mr. Mean did it," Nan reasoned. "He wanted her out of the way so he could search for the box."

"He must have been watching the house," Bert said, "and followed us to the lake. As soon as Danny tricked Freddie into saying where the box was, Mr. Mean led you and Freddie on a wild goose chase, then cut over to the road and hurried to a phone. He called Aunt Sallie and came here to watch until she left."

Nan smiled. "But he couldn't get in after all, because there wasn't any key under the mat."

Soon the older twins went to bed and fell asleep almost at once. In the middle of the night Nan was awakened by a loud banging. She put on her robe and slippers and stepped into the hall. The door to the boys' room opened, and Bert came out.

"That noise is coming from the attic," he said. "I guess one of the casements blew open."

"We'd better close it," said Nan.

They hurried down the hall, without bothering to turn on the bright light. When Bert opened the attic door, the noise suddenly stopped. He clicked on the light and went up the stairs, followed by Nan.

At the top, there was a door on each side of a hall and another at the end. On the right was Dinah and Sam's little apartment and the left one led into the playroom. The twins checked both places and found all the windows locked.

"Let's try the storage room," Nan said.

Bert led the way through the third door and turned on the light. The single bulb on the wall barely lit the big shadowy room.

"The windows are closed," he said.

"The latch must be broken on one of them," said Nan.

They examined each casement, then looked at each other in surprise. Nothing was broken! All of the windows were locked!

What had made the noise?

CHAPTER IX

THE DOLL HUNT

"BUT we heard a window up here banging!" Nan whispered.

Had someone opened, then closed the casement?

"We'd better search thoroughly," Bert said quietly.

The twins looked around the dimly lit attic. Propped against one wall were some old bedsteads. Beside them stood several large pictures in heavy gold-colored frames. Here and there were stacks of cartons.

The children walked across the bare wooden floor. One board squeaked.

"Flossie's burglar hit this!" Nan thought.

Bert and Nan looked behind the boxes and pictures. No one there!

"How about this trunk?" Bert asked.

They moved to a huge old-fashioned trunk in the middle of the room. Cautiously they lifted the lid. The trunk was full of linens. Quietly they put the top down again.

"What about that wardrobe?" Nan whispered. Her heart was thumping.

The large wardrobe was made of dark carved wood and had a mirror on one of its long double doors. While Nan held her breath, Bert walked over and pulled the metal door handles.

"It's locked," he said.

"There's no key either," Nan remarked, noting the empty keyhole. "Well, nobody's here. Let's go back."

Puzzled, the twins turned out the attic lights and went downstairs.

"Some other window must have been loose," said Bert. "Let's check."

Fifteen minutes later they had covered the whole house and were back in the upstairs hall. They had found everything locked.

"The wind was pretty strong. Maybe a branch was banging against the house," Nan suggested.

"Well—maybe," Bert said. Neither he nor his twin was satisfied with this explanation, but they did not know what else to think.

In the morning Nan was the first one up, and she dressed quietly. When she stepped out of her room, she heard Aunt Sallie calling her. Nan hurried into the guest room. The housekeeper was in bed under a heap of covers with her pink flannel nightgown buttoned up to her chin.

"I'm afraid I can't come downstairs, my dear," she said. "It's my lumbago. I can hardly move. I got it standing out in the cold last night."

"Oh, I'm so sorry," Nan exclaimed. "Shall we call the doctor?"

"My goodness, no!" Aunt Sallie replied. "I've had this often. I'll be fine again. All I need is a hot water bottle."

"I'll get you the heating pad," said Nan.

"No indeed!" said Aunt Sallie. "I'm not eating bad. My appetite is very good."

Nan smiled and repeated the sentence louder. After she had made Mrs. Pry comfortable, she said, "Don't worry about anything, Aunt Sallie. We'll take care of the house."

She hurried downstairs and soon had bacon sizzling on the stove and had mixed some waffle batter. Meanwhile the other children got up and dressed. After Flossie had taken a breakfast tray to Aunt Sallie, the twins ate their own breakfast.

"While Aunt Sallie's ill," said Nan, "everyone will have to help." She suddenly laughed. "Freddie, you have on one blue sock and one red one."

Flossie giggled. "Put on white shoes and you'll be Yankee Doodle Dandy!" Freddie went upstairs to change his socks.

When the morning chores were finished, Bert and the young twins went to church. Nan remained with Aunt Sallie. By the time the others came home, Nan had dinner ready.

"Did you cook all this?" asked Bert, surprised. "It's great!" Nan beamed.

Afterward Flossie and Freddie went to Aunt Sallie's room to make Valentines. Bert and Nan decided to call on Mrs. Villey. She had sold most of the curios.

Briefly Bert told her the story of Mr. Mean and asked if the weather toy they had bought was valuable.

Mrs. Villey shook her head. "Not especially."

"Then perhaps something was hidden inside the gingerbread house and that's why the man is so eager to get it," Nan suggested.

"No," said Mrs. Villey. "Last week I noticed that the roof was loose on the toy. I took it off and cleaned the whole thing carefully. I know nothing is hidden inside."

The twins looked disappointed. Their clue had failed!

Mrs. Villey went on, "My most valuable item was the Chinese mouse cage. But I had some bad luck with it. You remember the man who was here? He wanted to buy the cage, but one of the gold bells was missing. So he gave me a good deal less for it than I was hoping to get."

Nan looked surprised. "But I examined that cage just before he came," she said. "All the bells were on it. That man was putting something into his pocket when I found him. Maybe he took off the bell!"

Bert's eyes narrowed. "It sounds like something Mr. Mean would do."

Nan agreed. Then suddenly she remembered that the cage had fallen off the chair. She suggested that the bell might have come off then.

"Just to be sure, let's look for it," said Bert.

Mrs. Villey turned on all the lights, and the children examined the rug and the floor carefully. Bert wiggled on his stomach under a low velvet sofa. Suddenly he gave a muffled cry.

"Help! I'm stuck! Get me out!"

Nan took one of her brother's legs and Mrs. Villey the other. They tried to draw the boy out, but he was wedged tight.

"Pull harder!" Bert cried.

"It would be easier to lift the sofa," Nan said.

She and Mrs. Villey raised the heavy piece a few inches, and Bert scrambled out backward.

"Thanks," he said with a grin.

"Did you find the bell?" Nan asked.

"No."

"We've looked everywhere, then," said Nan. "It's not here. That Mr. Mean took it!"

"I didn't see a green muffler on him when we were here," Bert remarked, "but it might have slipped under his coat."

"He said his name was Kenny Blue," Mrs.

"Pull harder!" Bert cried. "I'm stuck!"

Villey told them. "He gave his address as the Happy Traveler Motel."

"That's a great clue!" exclaimed Bert. "We ought to report it to the police right away."

"Use my phone," said Mrs. Villey. "It's in the hall."

Bert talked to Chief Smith, then handed Nan her coat and took his own. "We must leave right now. Two officers are going to pick up Freddie and me at our house. We're going to the motel with them to identify the man."

The twins thanked Mrs. Villey for her help and went out. Nan said she wondered what Kenny Blue wanted with the weather toy.

"We'll soon find out," said Bert. "Now we know who Mr. Mean is and even where he lives. One of our mysteries is almost solved."

"But the play house secret isn't," Nan remarked.

"I know!" said Bert. "I think somebody doesn't want children hanging around the play house. Whoever it is, he also made the spooky moan and took the doll to frighten Flossie and her friends away. After all, there's no reason for anyone to want Flossie's rag doll. The person might even have thrown Hildy in the woods."

"That's an idea!" said Nan. "While you and Freddie go with the police, Flossie and I'll get Nellie and Susie and hunt for the doll."

Half an hour later the four girls were hurrying up to the Springer mansion. Nan was carrying a paper bag with a snack in it.

She rang the back doorbell. When the caretaker answered, Nan explained what they wanted to do. "And afterward we'd like to have a cocoa party in the play house, if you don't mind."

"It's okay," said Mr. Thurbell. "Just leave everything the way you find it."

With high hopes of locating the doll, Flossie and Susie hurried ahead and ran down the slope. Nellie said to Nan, "How are we going to see Hildy under all this snow?"

"I figure the person who took the doll got rid of her as soon as he could," Nan replied, "so we'll kick up all the snow we can around the play house and in the woods nearby. We might be lucky and find Hildy."

But an hour later they had not found the doll. Tired and discouraged, they returned to the play house.

"I'll make some cocoa," said Nan. "We'll have it with sugar cookies." She walked into the kitchen where she had left the brown paper bag.

"We need water for the cocoa," said Nan. "I guess we'll have to melt some snow."

"I'll get it in the kettle," Nellie offered.

"I'll help you," said Susie.

They went quickly to the front door. As Susie stepped outside, she stopped short with a gasp of fright. A man was peering into the window of the play house! With a startled cry, he turned and dashed off through the snow.

"Maybe he's the one who kidnapped Hildy!" Susie cried.

"Come on! Let's catch him!" Nellie urged.

The two girls dashed after the man, who raced across the little arched bridge. At the top he skidded, flailed his arms wildly and fell down the other side! The next moment the running girls hit the same patch of ice. Their feet flew out, and they slid down after him.

As they reached the bottom, the man rolled away. Susie seized him with one hand. Jerking free, he jumped to his feet and raced off into the woods!

"What happened?" called Nan, dashing out with Flossie.

Nellie jumped up and quickly explained.

"I got his scarf, though," called Susie. She proudly held up a green muffler!

CHAPTER X

MIXAMOO!

NAN'S heart pounded in excitement. Was the man who had looked in the window Mr. Mean? Was he connected with the play house mystery?

"What did he look like?" Nan asked, as Susie and Nellie crossed the creek toward her.

When they described him, Flossie said, "He was the same man I saw in our house!"

"What was he doing here?" Nellie asked.

"I don't know," said Nan, "but I'll bet he's the one who made the spooky moan and took Hildy to scare Flossie and Susie away."

"It's getting dark," said Susie, shivering. "I want to go home."

"All right," Nan agreed. "We'll have our cocoa party some other time."

Quickly the girls straightened the little kitchen. After each took a cookie, Nan put the refreshments in the paper bag and they left the play house. They waved good-by to Susie when they reached her home. At the Parks', Nellie said, "Don't worry about that man. Your brothers and the police will catch him when he goes back to his motel."

As Nan unlocked the Bobbseys' front door, Bert and Freddie came out of the living room.

"We didn't find the man," Freddie spoke up at once.

"When we got to the Happy Traveler Motel, Kenny Blue had checked out," Bert explained. "We rode around with the police to every other motel in the area, but Kenny Blue wasn't registered anywhere."

"He's probably using a false name," said Nan.

"You should have been with us," Flossie burst out. "Susie and Nellie almost caught him!"

She held up the green muffler.

The boys were amazed. "Where did you get this?" Bert asked.

Quickly the girls took off their coats and told their story.

Bert said, "Whatever Blue wants at the play house has something to do with that padlocked room, I'm sure."

"Let's go over to the play house now," Freddie said eagerly. "Maybe we could solve the mystery tonight."

"Good idea!" said Bert, and hurried to the telephone. "I'll ask Mr. Thurbell for permission to search."

Quickly he called information for the number of the Springer mansion. But when he dialed it, no one answered.

"Why don't you call the police and tell them about Mr. Mean and the play house?" Freddie asked eagerly.

"Because we're not absolutely sure the man was Mr. Mean," replied his brother.

"Besides, if we send the police there, we might get Mr. Thurbell in trouble with his employer," put in Nan.

The older twins decided they had better speak to the caretaker before going into the play house. Several times during the evening Bert called the mansion but there was no answer.

Just before bedtime, Flossie pressed her nose against the living room windowpane and looked out. "It's snowing again," she announced.

"And hard!" added Freddie. "Maybe there won't be any school tomorrow!"

"We won't be able to go to the play house either," said Flossie.

Next day Freddie was awake early. He hopped out of bed and ran straight to the window. "Wow!" he exclaimed.

A heavy blanket of snow lay over everything. Deep drifts had piled against the garage, covering Snap's doghouse entirely.

Quickly Freddie put on his slippers and robe and ran downstairs. As he switched on the television set, his brother and sisters hurried into the room. The newscaster announced that the Lakeport schools would be closed.

"We can play in the snow all day!" shouted Freddie.

When Nan ran upstairs to tell Aunt Sallie the news, she found the housekeeper was no better than before.

"I think we ought to send for the doctor," Nan said.

"No, no!" Mrs. Pry protested. "I have to be a lot worse than this before I bother with the doctor. The heating pad will do just fine. You'll see."

"All right," Nan said doubtfully. "I'll send Flossie up with your tray."

"We're really keeping house all by ourselves, aren't we?" said Flossie later as they cleared the breakfast table.

"Yes, and you're doing very well," Nan said. She handed an empty milk bottle to Freddie. "Put this on the back porch, please."

The little boy opened the door and started to go out.

"Yeow!" he yelled and stepped back. All the children burst out laughing. There was a wall of snow in the doorway!

"Talk about terrific drifts!" exclaimed Bert. "I'd better get the shovels from the basement!"

The twins put on snowsuits and boots and went out to dig. But as they worked, the wind blew the snow back again. Big flakes kept falling from the dark gray sky.

"It's no use," Bert said finally. "It's snowing faster than we can shovel. We may as well wait until the storm's over." They went inside and put the shovels away.

A few minutes later, Nan saw Bert standing in the hall, looking worried.

"What's the matter?" she asked.

"The play house must be deep in snowdrifts by now. We wouldn't be able to get in to search the attic even if Mr. Thurbell lets us."

"We ought to call him anyway," said his twin, "and tell him about seeing that man down there."

Bert nodded and picked up the phone. He waited for the dial tone. After a moment he pressed the button up and down and dialed a few numbers. Finally he gave up. "Our phone is dead."

"I guess some of the wires are down," Nan remarked.

At noon the twins had luncheon trays in the living room while watching the newscast. The announcer said that the storm was the worst in years. The local stores were closed. All planes and trains were canceled.

"Even if Uncle Ross is better, Mother and Dad couldn't get home," Bert said as he turned off the television.

The young twins looked downcast and soon wandered off to play.

"Let's slide down the banister," Flossie suggested. Eagerly they got their bed pillows.

Freddie put his on the banister, sat astride it and whizzed down backwards. "That's fun!" he called. "Come on!"

As he dashed up the stairs, Flossie slid down and bounced off at the bottom. Again and again they slid, more breathless and excited every minute. Soon they were racing each other to get to the top.

"It's my turn now," said Flossie, panting up behind Freddie.

"First come, first served!" he retorted.

"That's not fair!" exclaimed Flossie.

She threw her pillow over the banister and jumped on in front of him. As he pulled at her, she jerked free and swished down. But in her haste she had not thrown the pillow on straight. She felt it slipping.

"Help!" Off the banister she went, tumbled down two steps, and hit the table at the bottom!

Crash! A large vase fell to the floor and broke into a thousand pieces.

As Flossie began to cry, Nan came running from the kitchen and Bert from the living room.

"Help!" cried Flossie

"Are you hurt?" Nan asked as she helped Flossie up.

"My knee!" Flossie sobbed.

Nan looked at her sister's leg. "It's just scraped a little."

"What happened?" Bert asked Freddie.

"He pulled me," said Flossie with the tears streaming down her face.

"I did not!" said Freddie. "We were just fooling." Red-faced, he added, "Anyway, I didn't mean to hurt you. I'm sorry."

"You shouldn't play so rough," Nan said with a sigh. "Freddie, get the dustpan and broom and pick up that broken vase."

"I'll help you," said Bert. "Then you'd better shake out those pillows and put them back."

Nan led Flossie to the kitchen where she washed the little girl's knee and put a small bandage on it.

"I want Mommy." Flossie cried harder.

"There, there," said her sister. "Mother'll be home before you know it." Nan stifled a sigh and hoped she was right. Then she wiped Flossie's tear-stained face with a cool cloth.

When the boys came to the kitchen, Nan had poured glasses of milk for them and put a box of graham crackers on the table.

"Have a snack," she said, "and then I'll tell you a surprise." She smiled as she spoke, but her heart sank.

"What is it?" Freddie asked.

Nan took a deep breath. "We're going to have a very special supper. It's called Mixamoo."

Bert looked puzzled. "What does that mean?"

" 'Moo' stands for milk, and 'mixa' is what we're going to have with it."

"You mean we're not going to have regular meat and potatoes and dessert?" Bert asked.

"No. I just found out there aren't any in the house, and the stores are closed."

"I thought Mother and Dinah left lots of cold meats here and cookies and—" Bert spoke up.

"I did, too. But they're not here now. Anyway, we have lots and lots of milk and plenty of canned goods. So everybody can choose one can of something and we will mix them all together."

Flossie giggled in spite of her tears. "May we have pickles in the mixa?"

"Sure," said Nan recklessly. "Anything."

"That sounds like fun," said Freddie. He opened the food cupboard and looked over the canned goods. "I pick corn," he said.

"And I'll take baked beans," Flossie decided.

"Green beans for me," said Bert.

"And I choose Spanish rice," Nan added. "We'll stir it all together with ketchup and pickles."

By the time Aunt Sallie had a tray and supper

was on the table, the younger twins were in good spirits again.

Bert took a forkful of the Mixamoo. He rolled his eyes and grinned. "It's different."

"Aunt Sallie liked it," Flossie said.

"I do too," declared Freddie.

In a short time all the Mixamoo was gone. Nan heaved a sigh of relief.

The young twins went to bed early. Before the older ones followed they looked out the window and marveled at the snowdrifts, higher than any they had ever seen.

"We don't have to worry about intruders tonight," said Bert. "We can't get out, and no one can get in."

A short time later he was in bed, but did not go to sleep at once. Suddenly Bert sat up with a start. Did he imagine it, or was someone dialing the telephone in the lower hall?

CHAPTER XI

A MISSING CAKE

BERT jumped out of bed and hurried into the hall. Nan was just coming from her room.

"Did you hear someone using the phone?" she whispered.

"Yes."

The twins listened. All was silent.

"The phone isn't working," said Bert. "Maybe Snoop was playing with it."

"Just the same, let's go down and look," Nan suggested.

They turned on the lower hall light. No one was in sight. The twins went down the stairs and searched each room. They found no one. Snoop was curled up in his basket under the kitchen table near the heat. The door to the cellar was locked.

Finally Bert and Nan climbed the stairs. "I guess we're just getting jittery," Nan said.

In the morning the storm was over, and the

sun came out. The house, though, seemed very silent and dark.

"It's spooky," said Flossie as she and Freddie went downstairs to breakfast.

"That's 'cause the windows are covered with snow and ice," said Freddie. "We can't see out."

It was cheerful in the kitchen, though, when the light was turned on. Nan had breakfast ready.

"No school again today," Bert announced, coming in. "I heard the announcement on TV."

As Flossie was eating pancakes and syrup, she remarked, "Tomorrow's Valentine's Day. It's a good thing the storm's over or we couldn't have our party."

"The first thing we'll have to do is dig ourselves out, and then I'll go to the market," said Bert.

After breakfast he and the little twins washed the dishes, while Nan took a tray to Aunt Sallie.

"How do you feel?" she asked the housekeeper loudly.

"I can walk a bit," Aunt Sallie said, "but I know I still can't make the stairs." She looked worried. "You poor children. I'm no help to you at all."

"Don't feel bad, Aunt Sallie," said Nan. "We're getting along fine. But if you aren't better by this afternoon, I think we ought to have the doctor."

"No school!" Nan announced

"All right." The patient sighed. "But let's wait until then."

For the rest of the morning the twins worked hard clearing the sidewalk and making paths to the front and back doors. The neighbors were doing the same and soon there were narrow trails everywhere.

It was nearly noon when Bert hurried off to the supermarket. Freddie and Flossie started to build a snowman in the back yard.

They had just rolled a big ball for its head, when Snoop appeared on a snowdrift at the side of the garage. The cat walked back and forth, crying. Then he came over to Flossie and rubbed against her snowsuit.

Meow!

"What's the matter, Snoop?" she asked.

The cat ran up onto the well-packed drift and meowed again.

"What do you want?" Flossie asked, walking over to him with Freddie. Then a faint cry reached her ears.

"That sounds as if it's under the snow!" Freddie said.

The twins threw themselves on the drift and began to dig it away from the garage. Soon the roof of Snap's doghouse showed. The cries became louder and the children dug frantically. At last the entrance was free.

Freddie reached into the kennel and brought out a tiny ball of white fur.

"A kitten!" he exclaimed.

"Let's see!" said Flossie. She took the little animal from her twin. "This is Whitey!" she exclaimed. "She's one of Susie's kittens. I recognize her by her two black paws."

Snoop meowed loudly and rubbed against the children, his tail waving.

"Good cat! You saved the kitty!" said Freddie. He picked him up and followed Flossie, who carried the kitten into the kitchen to show their sister.

"Poor little thing!" Nan said, cuddling the kitten. "It probably crawled into Snap's house to get away from the storm and then was snowed in."

Nan heated milk for the two animals, as Flossie fondled the kitten. "I wish we could keep Whitey for a while," she said. "Maybe Susie would let us borrow her. I think I'll go over and ask her."

Meanwhile Bert was going through the check-out line in the crowded supermarket. After paying, he helped the clerk put the food into a large paper bag. A big chocolate cake went in last. It looked so good Bert could hardly wait to have a piece.

As he carried the bag out of the store, he

heard a loud whistle. Bert turned to see Danny and Jack crossing the parking lot.

"Hey, wait a minute!" Danny called. "I've got something to tell you."

Bert waited silently as the two boys came over, grinning. Danny had a big bag with peppermint sticks showing out of the top.

"What do you want?" Bert asked.

"You're in bad trouble, boy," said Danny and turned to Jack. "Isn't he?"

"I'll say."

"You could be in trouble yourself, Danny," said Bert coolly. "You'd better keep away from mean characters."

"I don't know what you're talking about," said Danny.

"I mean the fellow who gave you money at the lake the other day. I see you've been spending some of it," Bert added, eyeing the candy.

Danny grinned and popped a caramel into his mouth.

"How much did he give you for trapping Freddie with that question about the box?" Bert asked.

Danny shifted the candy to one side of his jaw. "None of your business."

"Who was that man? What did he say to you?"

Danny shrugged. "All I know is he said you had a box that belonged to him, but you wouldn't give it back. He told me what to say to Freddie and I said it. I don't know what it's all about and I don't care." He held up the bag of candy. "Thanks for the treat."

"Bert, you watch out," said Jack. "You're in for a hard time. Am I glad I'm not you!"

"What do you mean?"

"Suppose we won't tell you?" Jack taunted.

Bert turned away. "You don't know anything."

"Yes we do," said Danny quickly. "I heard that Mr. Harden called up from Florida and ordered his caretaker to collect the money for the broken deer from you right away."

"You'll have to think up a better one than that, Danny," said Bert in disgust. "You don't know anybody who knows Mr. Harden or the caretaker either."

Danny smirked. "You don't believe me? Okay. Just wait and see."

Bert walked on. When he reached home he went in the back door and placed the groceries on the kitchen table.

He found the other twins in the living room watching pictures of storm damage on television. Flossie was playing with Whitey. Quickly Freddie told his brother about finding the little kitten.

"Susie said Whitey ran out the back door yesterday," Flossie added. "She couldn't find her, and she was so worried. But she says we can keep her till Snap comes home."

"Snoop's a hero!" cried Freddie. "Yeah!" He grabbed the black cat and swung him around. With a yowl Snoop squirmed free and ran into the hall.

"Leave him alone," said Bert. "You know he doesn't like that." Then he told what Danny and Jack had said to him.

"I'm sure it's not true," said Nan.

Just then the TV announcer reported that planes and trains were beginning to move again, but were very crowded.

"I wonder how Uncle Ross is," said Nan.

"I wish Mommy and Daddy would come home," said Freddie.

"You'd better not count on it today or tomorrow," Bert warned.

Seeing that the young twins looked disappointed, Nan spoke up cheerfully. "Time for lunch! Let's see what Bert brought!"

The others followed her to the kitchen. As Bert started to unpack the grocery bag, he stopped short.

"Where's the cake?"

"What cake?" Nan asked.

"A chocolate cake. It was right here on top. I put it in myself."

"It must have dropped out," said Freddie.

His brother frowned. "I don't see how. The bag wasn't out of my arms all the way home."

"Are you sure you put the cake in?" Flossie asked.

"Positive."

Bert and Nan looked at each other. This was very strange!

"I'm hungry," Freddie said. "What else did you get?"

As the rest of the food was unpacked, the young twins forgot about the missing cake. But the others did not. After Aunt Sallie had been served, and the twins had eaten, Freddie and Flossie went into the living room.

At once Bert said to Nan, "I've been thinking about the cake disappearing, and probably other food. There's only one possible explanation."

"What is that?" Nan asked.

"We have an uninvited visitor in this house!"

CHAPTER XII

"HELP!"

"AN uninvited guest!" Nan cried in alarm.

"Yes, I think he stole the cake. How else could it disappear?" Bert asked. "I'm sure it didn't fall out of the bag on my way home from the market."

"Maybe you left the back door open and someone came in," said Nan. "Someone like Danny Rugg or Jack Westley."

"No. I closed the door, and it locks itself," her brother replied. "But I'll go outside and look for footprints that aren't ours."

He grabbed a coat and went out. Ten minutes later he was back. "No footprints," he reported.

Nan looked worried. "Bert, I've been thinking about our hearing someone at the telephone last night and all the food that's gone from the refrigerator. I think you're right about an uninvited guest hiding in the house."

Bert nodded. "It would be easy for him to take food. Every time all of us were in the living room, he could have sneaked down from the attic or up from the cellar and taken what he wanted."

"But why is he here?" Nan asked. "If he wants to steal something, why doesn't he just take it and leave?"

"In the storm he couldn't," Bert answered. "And don't forget, we've been in the house most of the time, and he hasn't had a chance to look."

Bert added, "I think we'd better search. Let's try to spot the fellow without letting him know. Then we'll call the police."

"First we'd better check the phone," said Nan. The twins hurried to the front hall and she picked up the instrument. After a moment Nan put it down. "Still dead."

"Then one of us will have to go for the police," Bert said.

"I don't want to scare Freddie and Flossie or Aunt Sallie," said Nan, "so we won't say anything until we're sure."

Bert agreed. "Let's start with the attic. That's where we heard the noise."

Quietly the two children went upstairs and opened the attic door. Avoiding the creaking step, they climbed to the third floor and tiptoed to the storage room. Silently Bert turned the knob and opened the door. For a moment they stared into the large shadowy room. No one was in sight.

Bert turned on the light. Staying together, the twins walked about softly, peering behind cartons and barrels and peering up at the rafters. They looked into the trunk and saw that the linens seemed undisturbed. Everything in the attic was the same, except that the big wardrobe doors came open easily.

"That's funny," said Bert. "It was locked before."

"Maybe it was just stuck," Nan suggested.

"You know what?" said Bert slowly. "I believe our visitor was hiding in here. When we tried the doors, he held them closed tightly."

Nan gave a shiver, "And to think we were right here!" she whispered.

The twins went on to search the playroom and Dinah and Sam's apartment. It was evident someone had been lying on the bed!

"He has probably left by now," Nan said. "We'd better see if our Valentine present is still in the closet, then go for the police."

The twins found the box in its hiding place, but on top some writing had been scratched out with black crayon. Nan and Bert looked at each other. The package appeared to have been opened!

Nan quickly unwrapped it. "It's the weather toy we bought," she said. "Do you suppose Flossie or Freddie took a peek?"

"Let's ask them, Nan. But why would they cross out the delivery name and address?"

Flossie and Freddie declared they had not opened the package nor been near the closet. The older twins did not tell them about the uninvited guest.

The telephone was still not working, so Bert went off to talk to the police. He told his story to Chief Smith, who was amazed.

"We'll send you home in a police car with two men who will go in to investigate."

There was no keeping this matter a secret from the young twins, who were full of questions. The police made a very thorough search but found no one.

Then one of them said, "My guess is that Mrs. Villey made two sales and packed each of them in boxes about the same size. Somehow she mixed them up and you were sent the wrong package. Someone else received yours and came here to exchange them. The name on this wrapping is the name of that customer. I'll take it to headquarters and try to figure it out."

The other policeman said, "The fellow went to a lot of trouble. He should have called up Mrs. Villey."

"Maybe he was afraid to," Nan ventured. "I think he might be the same man who took the bell off the cage at her shop."

"We're still trying to find him," the officer said. "Well, let us know if you have any more trouble."

After they had gone, Nan reminded Bert that they were going to tell Mr. Thurbell what had happened at the play house.

"I'll go," Bert offered.

As he hurried to the Springer mansion, he decided to ask Mr. Thurbell if Mr. Harden had called up from Florida. "I'm pretty sure Danny was making up that story," Bert thought, "but it's best to be certain."

Reaching the big yard, he walked down a path which had been shoveled to the back door. He rang the bell. No one answered. Bert tried several more times, but the caretaker did not appear.

"I guess he went shopping," Bert thought. As he turned to leave the back porch he noticed footprints and followed them to the front wall of the house near the iron deer. Snow was heaped up high around the edge of a hole. Bert knew the basement windows were below ground level and each had a concrete-lined space in front of it. Mr. Thurbell must have cleaned the snow away from this one. Suddenly a handful of snow came flying up out of the pit.

"Somebody's down there," Bert thought. He ran over and looked into the hole. There was Danny, trying to get out.

"What do you think you're doing?" Bert asked.

Startled, the bully glanced up. "I fell in," he replied.

Bert laughed. "What were you doing here?"

Danny said, "I—I was going to play a joke on the caretaker, that's all."

He started to climb out but fell back. He jumped up and tried a couple more times. The snow around him was too high, and the walls of the pit were slippery.

"It looks like the joke's on you," Bert said, grinning.

"Help me out of here!" Danny demanded.

"Sure I will," Bert said cheerfully, "just the way you helped Freddie when you pushed him into the cellar."

"Aw, come on," Danny wheedled.

Just then sharp barking sounded from the garage at the other side of the yard. It was followed by loud whimpers.

"Sounds like the dog's in trouble," said Bert.

"Forget about him!" Danny exclaimed. "Help me out of here!"

"I might do that," Bert said, grinning, "but first I'm going to see what's wrong with Rex."

As he walked away he heard Danny yelling angrily.

Inside the empty garage he found big Rex fastened to the wall by a chain. The dog had become entangled in it and each time he moved, the links pinched his front leg.

Bert approached cautiously. "Easy now, Rex," he said as the dog growled.

The boy felt in his pocket and found part of a chocolate bar. He unwrapped it and offered the candy to the dog. After carefully smelling it, Rex gobbled up the chocolate, then licked Bert's fingers.

"Good boy," Bert said softly. "Now stand still and let me help you." Carefully he unwound the chain. As soon as he was free, Rex gave a deep *woof!*

"That's okay. You're welcome," said Bert. "Now we're friends."

While fondling the animal, he wondered why Danny had come there. "Could he be looking for something?" Bert wondered.

Suddenly he remembered the ring Danny said he had lost. An exciting idea came to him. Suppose the bully had not lost it where he was throwing snowballs! Maybe the ring had gone sailing off *in* the snowball. Now it could be anywhere along the path.

"Even right by the deer," Bert thought.

"Help me out of here!" Danny demanded

"Be-ert!" Danny's cries started again. "Hurry up!"

With a final pat for the dog, Bert left the garage and strolled over to Danny.

Bert grinned down at him. "I really ought to leave you here for Mr. Thurbell to find."

"If you don't get me out of here, you'll be sorry!" Danny threatened.

Bert cleared away some of the snow around the pit, reached down and gave Danny his hand. The boy scrambled up. Without a word of thanks he ran off.

Bert kicked away a lot of snow from around the deer, hoping to find the ring, but did not see it.

"But I'll come back and look again," he told himself.

Suddenly he stopped short and stared straight at the iron statue.

"I wonder," he said, "if the ring hit the ear so hard it broke off a piece of it."

Bert began to hunt harder than ever.

CHAPTER XIII

TREE SPIES

EXCITED by his idea, Bert crouched and began picking up the snow around the deer.

"If I can prove that the ring broke the ear off this animal, then Danny will be to blame," he thought, "and not me!"

Little by little Bert sifted the snow through his fingers. He found pebbles, pieces of paper, even some ashes. But no trace of the ring. Finally the boy stood up and sighed.

"I guess I was wrong. I sure wish Mr. Thurbell would come back so I could find out if Mr. Harden did telephone from Florida."

Before going home Bert went down to the play house. He decided to take a look inside. Maybe the padlock would be off the closet in the attic, and he could peek inside!

To Bert's surprise the play house door was locked. Had Mr. Thurbell finally found the key to it?

"I'll try the windows," Bert thought.

Every one of them was locked. Furthermore, all the drapes had been pulled across them, so it was impossible to see inside.

"Hm," Bert mused. "Mr. Thurbell doesn't even want us to look in. I wonder why."

Suddenly another idea struck Bert. Suppose Mr. Thurbell had gone away and someone else was using the play house! He could have locked the door and drawn the curtains.

"Is he a good person or a wicked one?" Bert wondered. "I'd sure like to look into that padlocked closet."

He glanced up at the small attic window just below the peak of the roof. A stout branch of the maple tree hung near it.

"I can climb up there and look in!" Bert decided. Then he thought, "I couldn't see a thing without a flashlight. I'll get one and come back."

Excited, Bert hurried home. "Guess what?" he said to the other twins, and told them about the locked door and window.

"I want to go!" Freddie shouted.

Bert looked at Nan, who shook her head.

"Tell you what," he said. "Suppose we all go coasting, and just Nan and I will sneak over there. If everything's safe, we'll come and get you and Flossie."

The young twins thought this over. Finally Flossie said, "I can't go. Susie Larker's coming to play, and her mother's going to visit Aunt Sallie."

Freddie spoke up. "I sort of promised I'd go skating with Teddy Blake and his brother Ralph."

"That's cool," said Nan. "Then everybody's taken care of."

In a little while the Larkers arrived. "I had no idea you twins were having so much trouble and excitement," Susie's mother said. "I'll get your dinner."

"Thanks a lot," said Bert. "There's a rib roast in the fridge."

"Good. Everything will be ready when you get home."

Meanwhile Nan and Bert had been putting on their boots and coats.

"You stay as long as you want to," Mrs. Larker told them.

After Nan had thanked Susie's mother, the older children left. They went to the garage to pick up their sleds. Bert took a flashlight from the shelf and stuck it in his pocket. Then the twins hurried toward the big hill.

"Shall we coast first or play detective?" Nan asked her brother.

"Let's take a few rides," said Bert, "and then go to the play house."

After whizzing down the slope several times, the two Bobbseys crept through the break in the hedge.

"Let's try Mr. Thurbell once more," Nan suggested.

Leaving their sleds in front of the play house, they hurried up the steep incline toward the mansion. Although the afternoon was beginning to grow dark, no light showed in the house.

"We'll ring the bell anyway," said Bert. Several times he pushed the button and waited. "I guess Mr. Thurbell isn't home yet."

"I can't wait to get a look in the attic window of the play house," said Nan. "Let's go back."

The children trudged down the hill.

"How are we going to get up on the roof to look in that window?" Nan asked. "Climb the tree?"

"Sure. It'll be easy."

He led the way to the big maple beside the play house. Bert shone his light on the trunk and saw a few old boards nailed crossways to make a ladder. He tested one with his foot.

"They're pretty rotten, but they'll help a little," he said.

Grabbing the trunk, he managed to scramble onto a low branch. Then he reached down and helped Nan up. The children crawled higher to the wooden platform. Bert saw that it was made of heavy boards.

"This'll hold us," he said, feeling his way onto it. Nan followed.

"You wait here, and I'll—"

Bert broke off suddenly. In the distance Rex began barking frantically. From their high perch the twins could see two men coming down the hill.

"Who are they?" Nan asked softly.

"I can't tell," said Bert. "They're too muffled up." The two had soft hats pulled low, and their overcoat collars were turned up to their eyes against the biting wind.

Nan looked worried. "One's just about that Kenny Blue's size," she said.

Bert nodded. The other man was taller.

"What if they see us here?" whispered Nan.

Bert looked grim. "Just hope they don't look up."

Suddenly Nan gasped. "Our sleds!"

Bert exclaimed in dismay, "We must get them!"

"But there's no time!" Nan said, glancing at the two men plodding toward the play house.

"We'll have to risk it," said her brother, already swinging down through the tree. "Stay here!"

Nan watched anxiously as he ran along the side of the play house and stepped around to the front.

"Oh, hurry, Bert!" Nan was saying as she saw

the two men approaching along the opposite side of the little house.

Bert grabbed a sled in each hand and ran around the corner just as the men rounded the front. Silently the boy handed the sleds up to Nan, who stuck one in the nearby branches. Then she clambered to the platform and thrust the other one into the limbs above her. Moments later Bert reached the lookout spot, panting. He settled down and gave a sigh of relief.

The two men had paused by the play house door. The shorter one was feeling in his pocket. Suddenly a sharp gust of wind shook the tree. The sled above the twins slipped and fell. With a gasp Nan grabbed for it. But it hit the platform with a clatter.

"What was that?" asked the big man in a deep voice.

His companion answered softly. The words were muffled into the turned-up collar of his coat.

"Come on," said the tall man. "We'd better take a look around. Maybe it's those nosy kids you were telling me about."

The two men walked around the side of the play house.

"Nobody's here," said the shorter man, shivering. "Let's go inside."

"I heard a noise," said the other one stubbornly, "and I'm going to find out what it was.

Besides, we saw footprints coming down the hill, and they're all around here."

"Probably the caretaker's," said the smaller man.

The pair continued to circle the house.

"All right," said the big man when they reached the front again. "I guess it was the tree branches hitting together in the wind."

Once more the smaller man dug deep in his pocket. His friend frowned.

"Don't tell me you've lost the keys!" he growled. "It wouldn't surprise me, though, if you had. You let one valuable item slip through your hands. It's a good thing that you got it back."

The smaller man muttered something which the children could not understand, then brought out the key. He unlocked the door and led the way into the play house. The twins heard the front door close. A few moments later a light streamed onto the snow from the attic window.

"Now's our chance!" Bert exclaimed softly. "I can get a really good look while that light is on."

"But don't let them see you," said Nan in a worried voice.

"I'll be okay," Bert whispered. "Here I go! Don't let the sled slip."

Carefully he left the platform and climbed out along a stout limb which overhung the

Bert lost his balance

house. He lowered himself gently so that he was kneeling astride the roof peak. Then he inched his way along the snowy ridge to the front of the house. Leaning over the edge, he tried to look into the attic.

"The window is too far down," he thought. Pulling himself forward a little more, he leaned over farther. Suddenly a hard wind shook the tree and slapped a big branch against the roof.

Startled, Bert sat up suddenly and lost his balance. He gave a sharp cry and tumbled from the roof. The next moment a mound of snow dropped off the play house and covered him.

"He's buried in the snow!" Nan thought. "I'll have to get him out!"

But at that moment the light went off in the play house. Crouched on the platform, Nan watched anxiously.

In a few moments the door opened, and the two men came out. They circled the house.

"I don't see anybody," said the smaller man. "We're safe."

"I heard somebody yell," the big man insisted. "If those kids are here, I'm going to find 'em!"

Then he added harshly, "I'd like to get my hands on them!"

CHAPTER XIV

A SEARCH

NAN looked down through the branches as the two men searched around the play house. She hardly dared breathe.

"I heard somebody yell," the tall man said. "And I'm going to find out who it was."

Nan was worried. "I hope Bert doesn't try to get out of the snow right now," she thought.

With the smaller man trailing behind, the big fellow walked right past where Bert had fallen. The mound of snow remained still! Nan sighed in relief.

After the men had circled the play house, the tall one said, "There's nobody here. Now that I've seen what's in the attic we may as well go."

He locked the door, and the two men started toward the slope.

"This way! I don't like that dog!" said the smaller one.

He took the lead, and they followed the frozen stream into the woods. Instantly Nan scrambled to a lower limb and dropped down. She ran to her brother.

"Bert! Come out! It's safe!"

At once snow began to fly from the mound that covered him, and soon Bert popped up.

Despite herself, Nan giggled as he climbed out. "You look like a snowman."

Bert shook himself. "I started to come up, but I figured they heard my yell, so I decided to stay put. I dug a little hole for air, but I'm glad I didn't have to stay there any longer."

"Did you look in the window before you fell?" Nan asked.

"No. Where did the men go?"

"Into the woods."

"Let's trail them," Bert suggested. "Maybe we can find out where they're going and give the police a lead."

"But I'm not sure the smaller man was Mr. Blue," Nan said.

"I'm not certain either," her twin replied, "but we know he looked like him. Let's try to find them anyway."

By this time the sun had set. Bert turned on his flashlight and they followed the frozen creek bed into the woods. The men were not in sight.

Suddenly just beyond a bend in the creek the children heard the crackling of brush. Quickly Bert turned off his light and the twins stood still.

"Ouch!" came a loud cry. There was a sound of more brush breaking.

The children inched forward and peered around the curve. The big man was on his knees, muttering angrily.

"Get me up!" he exclaimed as the other tried to pull him to his feet. "This is your fault!"

"How come?"

"I fell over a beaver dam! That's what we get for walking in the creek bed. You should have known better!"

"I'm sorry, Hard," replied his companion quietly.

The men left the stream and went off among the trees.

The twins, amazed at what they had heard, looked at each other. "Did you hear that?" Nan whispered. "The man we think is Mr. Blue called him Hard."

"I know. Do you think that's short for Harden?"

"If it is, he has every right to go to the play house," said Nan, "and we have *no* right to spy on him."

"That's true," Bert agreed gloomily. "Whatever is in the attic is none of our business. We certainly can't report the men as prowlers."

The twins stood shivering in the cold wind, thinking this over.

"Still, we know Mr. Blue is not honest," Nan said, "so maybe we should tell the police what happened anyhow."

Bert agreed. "But first, let's see if we can find out where they're going. Then we can tell the police that."

Using Bert's light, the twins followed the men's tracks through the deep snow in the woods. After a while the trees grew thinner and the trail came out on a paved road.

"There they are!" said Nan, pointing across the street.

Lights from a store window showed the two men boarding a bus. As it drove off Nan noted that it went toward the center of town.

"That doesn't tell us much," Bert remarked. "I guess we'd better go on home. It must be past suppertime."

"We have to go back for our sleds," Nan reminded him.

With the help of Bert's flashlight, the twins made their way quickly through the woods. By now their desire to solve the play house mystery had become strong again. Nan suggested that her brother go up on the roof and look in the attic window.

"Since we don't know for sure who the men are, we shouldn't pass up this chance to solve the mystery."

Bert agreed and climbed up. When he flashed his light into the window, all he could see was a flat brown surface.

"No use. A box or something has been moved in front of the window," he remarked. Then he climbed over to the tree and handed the sleds down to Nan.

The children pulled them up the slope and past the mansion. There were still no lights in it.

When Nan and Bert reached their own house, lights were burning cheerily. A welcoming aroma of cooking meat filled the air.

"You're just in time!" Flossie called out. "Susie's mother made us an angel cake high as a mountain."

Bert laughed. "Guess I'd better start climbing it now!"

Nan and Bert thanked Mrs. Larker. "That's all right," she said kindly, putting on her coat. "If you need anything else tonight, give me a call." She kissed Nan and the young twins, gave Bert a pat on the shoulder and left with Susie.

During dinner Freddie and Flossie were told about the men at the play house.

"I wish you'd caught them," said Freddie.

"Yes," Flossie added. "That bad man who scared us is too mean to be around."

When they finished eating, Bert went to the telephone. He tried Mr. Thurbell's number. No answer. He dialed police headquarters and told the captain on duty about the men and the play house.

"We'll investigate it," the officer promised.

As Flossie was helping her sister in the kitchen, Nan noticed that Flossie looked worried. And she was quiet most of the evening. Near bedtime the little girl went over to the big chair where Nan sat reading and cuddled next to her.

"Where do you suppose Hildy is?" Flossie asked sadly.

"I guess she's all right," said Nan, patting Flossie's knee. "Probably she's sitting in a nice comfortable chair just the way we are."

"I wish she was here," said Flossie a little shakily. "I liked to take her to bed with me."

"Why don't you find something else? How about your teddy bear?" Nan asked.

"I know what!" Flossie exclaimed. She sat up straight. "I'll take the kitty. May I please, Nan? Please?"

The older girl looked doubtful. "Mother doesn't usually let you take Snoop to bed."

Flossie giggled and looked at the big cat curled up near the radiator. "Oh, I don't mean him. He wouldn't go. Snoop likes to sleep by himself."

"Then what did you mean?" Nan asked.

"I mean the baby kitty—Susie's kitty."

"All right," said Nan.

"Oh, thank you!" Flossie exclaimed. "I'll get her right away. She's in her box in the basement."

Half an hour later the young twins were tucked in bed, and Whitey was curled up alongside Flossie. A little later Nan quietly went to bed in the room she and Flossie shared.

"How sweet Flossie and the kitten look!" she thought.

Sometime later the little girl awoke. It took her several seconds to realize what was the matter.

Whitey was gone!

"Oh dear, I must find her. She'll catch cold!" Flossie thought.

She jumped out of bed and turned on a lamp. The little girl blinked a few times, then started to hunt for the kitten. She looked under the two beds, the bureau, desk, and each chair. Whitey was not there.

Suddenly Flossie cried out, "Oh!"

The noise, together with the light, woke Nan. "What's the matter, Flossie?" she asked.

"Lots of things. Nan, Mr. Mean—I mean Mr. Blue's green scarf is gone! It was hanging right here on this chair. And the kitty's gone! Oh, Nan, he must have been in here and taken both of them!"

Nan leaped from the bed. At the same time she noticed the door to the hall was open.

"Flossie, did you open the hall door?"

"No, Nan." She too looked across the room. "Mr. Blue did it!"

Her sister was really alarmed now. She rushed into the hall. Every bedroom door and the one to the attic was open!

Nan stood still. "Nan Bobbsey, get hold of yourself!" she scolded.

Nan wanted to call Bert but hated to waken him. "Maybe the kitten pushed the doors open," she told Flossie, "and dragged the scarf with her. Let's look."

This made the little girl feel better and she followed Nan. Softly they called, "Here kitty, here kitty!"

Whitey did not appear, and Flossie again said perhaps Mr. Blue had taken her and the scarf. To keep her from worrying, Nan suggested they look in the attic. But it still seemed strange to her that every door was partly open.

She also noticed something else: One of Freddie's old hook-and-ladder toys stood near the top of the stairs.

"Funny," Nan thought. "Why did he leave it there? And it's the special antique one Cousin Martha gave him a couple of years ago." She decided to move the old toy when the two girls came back downstairs.

They hurried along the hall and started to mount the steps to the attic. Nan felt for the

"It's spooky," said Flossie

switch and flicked it, but the light did not go on.

"I guess the bulb's burned out," she said. "I'll get my flashlight."

She brought it from her bedside table. Then they climbed up. The attic light did not work either.

The cat was not in the hall. The girls looked in the two rooms. Finally they made their way to the open door at the end. Nan flipped the light switch. Nothing happened.

"Oh, it's spooky having all the lights out," said Flossie.

Nan swept her flashlight beam over the big storage room.

"Here, kitty!" Nan called softly, and Flossie called her too.

The girls walked toward the center of the room, moving the light along the floor.

"Maybe she went under the wardrobe," said Flossie softly.

The two sisters stepped up to the mirrored door. Nan's flashlight showed the reflection of the big trunk behind them. The next instant its lid started rising! A big white thing rose out of it flapping and came straight toward them!

CHAPTER XV

LOST AND FOUND

SCREAMING, Nan and Flossie dashed to the attic stairs and raced down them to the second floor hall. The noise awakened Bert and Freddie and even Aunt Sallie.

"What's the matter?" Bert cried, running from his room.

Freddie came out too and then Aunt Sallie. When she heard "ghost in the attic" and "it's after us," she herded all the children into her room and shut the door.

Clicking on a lamp, she said, "Now I want the full story."

Before it could be told, Flossie squealed, "There's Whitey!" She rushed over to an armchair where the kitten had cuddled partly under a pillow. "Oh, that bad man didn't steal you!" She picked up the warm, furry little thing and hugged her.

By now Nan had told about the trunk ghost. Aunt Sallie's eyes flashed. "This spookiness has gone far enough. Come, we'll investigate!" Her lumbago suddenly seemed to be cured.

She opened the door to the hall and looked around. No ghost or other person was there. Aunt Sallie started for the attic.

"Wait a minute!" Nan shouted. She was staring toward the front stairway. "Freddie's antique hook-and-ladder's gone!"

"What do you mean?" the little boy exclaimed.

Nan told him, and at once Freddie ran into his room to look. He gave a loud cry. "My very favorite special hook-and-ladder!" he wailed.

"This means the ghost went down the front stairs," said Bert, dashing toward the steps.

"And probably out the front door," Nan added.

"Good riddance!" Flossie spoke up.

Nan was right. Two white sheets lay near the front door. The toy hook-and-ladder and the green scarf were gone.

"And don't forget Hildy," Flossie added.

"My, my," said Aunt Sallie, "I never heard of so many mysteries in just a few days. I'm going to call the police, and then tomorrow we'll put bolts on all our doors. Locks don't seem to keep out that Mr. Blue."

"And I'll make hot cocoa right now for all of us," Nan offered. "Then we can go to bed again."

Two policemen arrived shortly and made another thorough search. They found nothing beyond what the children knew.

"We will have a man watch your house until you put on the bolts," one of them said. "And don't worry."

"Officer," Nan asked, "did you ever figure out what name was under the one that was scratched off our package?"

"Yes, we did, but it didn't help us much," he answered.

"What was it?"

"Blue."

"Blue!" the twins chorused, and Bert added, "That means Mrs. Villey got the wrong names on the packages. Mr. Blue opened his right away and figured we had the mouse cage he'd bought."

"And came to get it," Freddie shouted.

"Right," said the officer.

Flossie giggled. "And got snowbound with us and had to steal our food."

The children finally got to bed but were up early the next morning. There was more snow. Again the Lakeport schools would be closed.

"Does everybody remember what today is?" said Nan at breakfast.

They thought a moment, then Flossie exclaimed, "It's Valentine's Day! Oh dear, can't we have our party?"

Bert looked out. "It isn't that bad. See, people are walking in the street. As soon as I do some shoveling, I'm going over to Springer's."

"Why?" Freddie asked.

Bert grinned. "I have a hunch about the snowball that broke off the deer's ear. Tell you later if I'm right."

The others coaxed him to reveal his secret, but Bert changed the subject. "Nan, let's give Freddie and Flossie their Valentine now."

"Okay."

"I'll get it," Bert offered and went upstairs.

He brought it down and set the box on the table. At once the young twins began to tear off the paper.

"Untie the cord first," said Nan.

Aunt Sallie looked a little worried. "I hope it won't roar and burst too far."

The children giggled and Nan repeated what she had said. Aunt Sallie laughed. "Oh dear, cord—roared—first—burst—I must get my hearing aid fixed."

By this time the box was opened, and Freddie lifted out the Valentine toy.

"Oo, it's bee-yoo-ti-ful!" cried Flossie.

"How does it work?" Freddie asked.

Bert showed them the way the witch came out

in bad weather, and Hansel and Gretel when it was clear. Right now the witch stood in front of the door.

"I s'pose the witch chases the rain clouds away with her broom," Flossie remarked, and the others laughed.

"This house," said Freddie, "isn't made of real gingerbread. You can't eat it."

"That's right," Nan agreed. "It's wood, and you'd better not put your teeth in it. Or let Snap when he comes home."

At this moment Snoop came walking into the room, stretched, then jumped onto a chair by the table. Without warning he put his front paws up on one side of the house and began to scratch it with his nails.

"Snoop! Stop that!" Flossie scolded and shooed the cat off the chair.

There was one bad scratch but Aunt Sallie brought some polish and the mark was soon gone. Freddie and Flossie decided to set the toy among some plants on a shelf at one of the dining room windows.

"Look!" Flossie cried. "The witch is starting to walk inside! It's going to be clear!"

The twins watched fascinated as the little figure slowly jerked along carrying her broom. She went inside and the door closed.

In a couple of moments music began to play. The other door opened. Hansel and Gretel danced outside, then stood still. Presently the music stopped.

"Wow, that's really cool," said Freddie. "Thanks a lot, Nan and Bert."

"Yes, thank you," Flossie added. "And now I want to give out my Valentines."

She hurried upstairs. Freddie followed, saying, "I have some too."

Soon Nan, Bert, and Aunt Sallie had their presents. Freddie had given each of them a red heart cinnamon lollipop. Flossie had made little animals out of spools of brown thread for Nan and Aunt Sallie. Freddie received a candy heart. For Bert, Flossie had a real surprise—she had had his favorite penknife mended.

"That's great," he said.

There were many kisses and thank-you's, then Nan said, "Flossie, you and I had better start getting ready for the party."

"Freddie and I will shovel," Bert told her.

An hour later he started for the Springer mansion. On the way he bought bolts for the Bobbseys' doors, then hurried up the street. He rang the Springer front doorbell. When there was no response Bert walked to the rear of the house. The back door stood open.

"Hello, Mr. Thurbell," he called.

When the caretaker did not come, Bert took off his boots, stepped into the kitchen, and called again.

"Down here!" came a voice. Bert saw the open door leading to the cellar steps. "I've got furnace trouble," called Mr. Thurbell. "I can't come up. Who is it?"

The boy closed the outside door and hurried over. "It's Bert Bobbsey, Mr. Thurbell. I have to ask you something important. Is Mr. Harden home?"

"Not that I know of," the caretaker replied.

"May I come down?" said Bert. "I have lots to tell you."

"Come ahead."

Bert told Mr. Thurbell how many times he had tried to reach him.

"My phone hasn't been working," he replied, "and I've been out a lot."

"Did you lock the play house door?" Bert asked.

"Why, no."

Bert gave him all the details about the two men who had been there with a key. "One called the other Hard. We thought maybe he was Mr. Harden."

"I'm sure it wasn't," Mr. Thurbell said. "I don't expect him until next week. If he flew up early, why wouldn't he come here?"

Bert shrugged and said, "Mr. Thurbell, would you go down to the play house with me?"

"Sure. Wait'll I wash my hands and get my coat."

When they reached the mysterious little house, the caretaker tried the door. It was locked. He frowned.

"I can't understand this."

He took a large keycase from his pocket and tried one key after another. At last Mr. Thurbell found one that fitted. He opened the door and they walked in. Everything looked the same on the first floor, so they climbed to the attic. The padlock on the closet was in place.

Mr. Thurbell began trying his keys on it, but this time he had no luck. Meanwhile Bert's eyes had been searching the floor for a possible clue to the strange men. Suddenly he jumped forward.

"Look! A clue! I'll bet this is Freddie's ladder!"

"What do you mean?" Mr. Thurbell asked.

Bert explained about the stolen antique hook-and-ladder. "It belonged to my little brother. I'm sure the rest of the toy is inside this closet."

"You said you've already told the police about Hard and Blue," Mr. Thurbell remarked. "Suppose you take this little ladder home. If your brother can identify it, then I suggest you take it to the police."

They went downstairs. The caretaker locked the door, then unhooked the key from the case. "Bert, will you take this to a locksmith and have two more made? Give one to the police and keep

"Look! A clue!"

the other yourself. Go in the play house any time." Mr. Thurbell smiled. "You're a good detective."

"Can you take a little more time?" Bert asked.

"Sure. What is it?"

Bert reminded Mr. Thurbell that the mystery of who had broken off the ear of the iron deer on the front lawn had never been solved.

"That's right, Bert. I was waiting for Mr. Harden to come home."

"Maybe we won't have to wait that long," said Bert.

He led the way to the deer. "I thought perhaps—" the boy began, then stopped. He was gazing down into a small hollow where the ear had broken off.

"Yes?" said Mr. Thurbell, puzzled.

"I think perhaps something hard in a snowball hit the deer. Maybe whatever it was fell down inside this hollow," the boy answered.

The caretaker nodded. "That's possible. Do you see anything?"

"It's too dark."

"Suppose I get a flashlight, Bert."

"Just a minute. I'll try to reach in."

Bert pulled off his right glove and put his hand into the hollow. His fingers felt two hard objects.

CHAPTER XVI

BAIT FOR A BULLY

BERT hardly dared believe his guess had been correct about the deer.

"Is something there?" Mr. Thurbell asked, as the boy continued to feel in the hollow of the broken-off ear.

"Ye-es," Bert answered. "Two things. I think one of them is what I'm looking for."

Again and again he tried to grasp the object between his fingers so he could lift it up. Each time it would slip away. The hole was not large enough for him to make a fist and hold onto his prize.

"What is it you're looking for?" the caretaker asked finally.

"A ring," Bert replied. "You remember another boy was throwing snowballs when I was? He lost a ring. I think it came off in the snowball."

Mr. Thurbell reached into a pocket. "Maybe this will help you," he said. "It's a magnet."

"Boy, that's cool," Bert cried.

He took the magnet. In a few seconds it came out of the hole, grasping a silver-colored ring. Bert found the secret spring and the top flew up. Inside were scratched the initials DR.

"What does that stand for?" Mr. Thurbell asked.

"Danny Rugg."

The caretaker took the ring and balanced it on the palm of one hand. "This doesn't weigh much," he remarked. "I don't see how it could have had enough force to break the deer."

Suddenly Bert put his hand down into the hollow again. He felt for the other object. After several tries, his fingers finally managed to grasp it.

"A stone!" Mr. Thurbell cried.

He and Bert stared at it, then at each other. "This could have broken off the ear!" Bert exclaimed.

"Right. Danny must have put it inside his snowball. That's the only way it could have rolled into the opening," Mr. Thurbell declared.

Bert said nothing but he recalled seeing Danny turn his back and lean over toward the ground just before making the snowball he threw.

"Where does this Danny Rugg live?" Mr. Thurbell asked. He seemed angry now.

When Bert told him, he said, "I'm going there right away to talk to him or his parents. Bert, I'd like you to come along."

"All right," Bert agreed, although he would have preferred not to.

"You won't have to take any blame for being a tattletale," the man told him. "I'll do the talking."

Mr. Thurbell got his car, and they drove off. Mrs. Rugg answered the bell. Bert introduced the caretaker.

"I'd like to talk to you and your son," Mr. Thurbell said. "I have his ring."

"Oh, you found it? Good! Come right in." She opened the door wider. Then she called up the stairs, "Danny, you have callers."

She led the visitors into the living room, and they all sat down. In a moment they heard Danny coming.

"Oh!" he exclaimed upon seeing Bert.

"This is Mr. Thurbell from the Springer mansion," Mrs. Rugg told her son. "He has a surprise for you."

Bert watched Danny's face carefully. He was going to get a big surprise all right!

Mr. Thurbell took the ring and the stone from his pocket. "I believe these belong to you, Danny."

When Danny saw the ring, he smiled. "Gee, thanks. I 'm glad you found—" Suddenly he looked at the stone. "I—what—this isn't mine."

The caretaker said angrily, "The ring and the stone were found together in a little hollow where the ear broke off the deer. You put the stone in a snowball that hit the deer. Why did you do it?"

"I thought it would make the snowball go faster than Bert's," Danny confessed before he had a chance to think.

Mrs. Rugg spoke up. "Danny, I'm shocked. You told me Bert knocked the ear off."

Danny hung his head. "Bert Bobbsey makes me sick."

Mrs. Rugg turned to Mr. Thurbell. "My husband will pay for the damage, of course, but Danny will have the money taken out of his allowance."

"I don't get enough for that!" Danny exclaimed.

"You can pay some each week," his mother said.

"It'll take forever!" the boy cried angrily.

"Listen, Danny," said Mrs. Rugg, "if you'd only broken the ear, your father would have paid all or at least part of it, because accidents do happen. But you didn't play fair using a stone, and you let someone else be accused.

That's a very dishonest thing to do, and that's why you're being punished."

Danny's chin began to tremble, and he stomped to the window.

Mrs. Rugg sighed. "I'm sorry, Bert," she said. "And send us a bill, Mr. Thurbell."

A few minutes later Bert stopped at the locksmith's, then he went home. Instantly the twins crowded around him.

"Was your hunch right?" Nan asked.

"Was it!" Bert exclaimed. "And paid off double. Listen to this."

When Freddie heard how Bert's detective work had turned the tables on Danny, he shouted, "Yeah!" jumped over the sofa, and did a double somersault across the floor.

Flossie clapped her hands, and Nan said, "That was cool, Bert."

Bert now brought the toy ladder from his pocket. "Freddie, did this come off your old hook-and-ladder?"

The little boy examined it, then shouted, "It sure did. Where'd you find this?"

His brother explained. "And I think the rest of your toy is in that locked closet. Mr. Thurbell wants me to take this to the police. I'll be right back."

Bert hurried off but was not gone long. After an early lunch he said, "Freddie, I brought three bolts for our doors. Want to help me put them on?"

"Sure. But let me put one on all by myself. I know how," Freddie insisted.

"Okay."

Bert handed the little boy a lock and screws. Freddie hurried off to get an awl to make holes for the screws, and his own special screwdriver.

"I want to take the kitchen door," he told Bert, who was already at work on the front door. Later Bert would bolt the side door, where steps led down to the basement.

As Freddie worked, Aunt Sallie watched him and thought, "How well he's doing for such a small boy!"

Snoop kept rubbing against Freddie and interfering with his work. "Go away, Snoop!" he ordered. "I almost put this hole in the wrong place."

The cat refused to leave, so Freddie forgot him. Soon he had finished his job, but something was wrong. When he pushed the bolt, nothing happened. He asked Aunt Sallie to take a look, but she could not figure out the trouble.

Just then Bert walked in. Freddie asked him.

Suddenly his older brother began to laugh. "It won't work because you've put it on upside down and backwards!"

"Golly," said Freddie, "you mean everybody

has to stand on his head to lock and unlock this door?"

"I guess that's right, Freddie. Want to be the first one to try it?"

Freddie did just that with his feet braced against the door. "Hm," he said, getting up. "Upside down locks aren't so good. I'll have to take it off, Bert, and put it on right."

"Good idea, old sport," said Bert. "While you do it, I'll put the bolt on the basement door."

The two boys had just finished when Nan and Flossie came downstairs dressed for the Valentine party. "Freddie and Bert, you'd better go change your clothes," Nan advised. "The kids'll start coming pretty soon. But wait just a second. I thought of something special to add to the party."

"What is it?" Bert asked.

"I'll bet it's another game," Freddie guessed.

"Sort of, yes."

"Hurry up and tell us," Flossie begged.

Nan explained that she and Bert wanted to do some more hunting at the play house. "How about making a detective game out of it? Bert and I will go first, then Freddie and Flossie and all the others can follow."

"What'll we do?" Freddie asked. "It sounds neat."

"Bert and I will go inside."

"Upside down locks aren't so good," said Freddie

"And take the padlock off the mystery room," Bert added. "I've figured out how to do it."

Nan went on, "Maybe Mr. Hard and Mr. Blue will come, and we'd like to capture them."

"Oo, it sounds scary," Flossie spoke up.

"You won't come in the house," Nan said. "All of you will hide behind trees and bushes and piles of snow."

"But how are we going to capture the bad men?" Freddie asked.

Nan said, "If you see them coming, go get Mr. Thurbell and tell him to call the police."

"Oh this is 'citing!" Flossie exclaimed.

"After our friends get here," Nan added, "I'll tell them."

"You mean give everybody a special job?" Freddie asked. "I want to be—to be Detective Frederick."

The others laughed, then the boys hurried upstairs to dress. Nan and Flossie walked around to check on the party preparations.

"It's bee-yoo-ti-ful!" Flossie exclaimed, as she gazed at the living room mantel.

Nan had put flowers and plants on it. Stuck among them were pure white paper cupids on sticks.

The dining room table was set with a red paper cloth and napkins. A covered platter of sandwiches stood on it and dishes of nuts and special Valentine candies. Aunt Sallie had made two angel cakes with red icing and decorated them with candy arrows.

"Nellie's coming early," Nan said. "She's bringing a special red heart to hang on the light over the table. Oh, there's the bell. Maybe that's Nellie."

As the girls reached the front door, Bert and Freddie ran downstairs.

"Wait!" said Freddie. "Let's guess who's first. I think it's Teddy."

"Charlie."

"Susie."

"Nellie."

Nan opened the door. "We're all wrong."

The parcel post man stood there. He was holding a large package.

Smiling, he said, "Here's a Valentine surprise for the Bobbsey Twins. Be careful. It says, 'HANDLE WITH CARE. DIRECTIONS INSIDE.' "

CHAPTER XVII

SNOOP'S TRICK

NAN had already looked at the sender's name. "It's from Mother and Daddy!" she exclaimed. "Oh, what fun!"

The parcel post man left the eager children and went off to his truck. Nan closed the door and the twins carried the package into the living room. Soon it was open.

"A toy donkey!" Freddie shouted.

"It's made of paper," Flossie added.

Nan lifted the donkey from the tissue around it. A red heart was tied to its neck and there was another red ribbon trailing underneath.

"I guess you're s'posed to hang it up," Flossie said. "Where shall we put our donkey Valentine?"

Bert had noticed that the heart was a double card. He unfolded it.

"Listen!" he ordered. "This says, 'Happy

Valentine's Day to our lovely twins. Hang up this *piñata* from Mexico. When all your guests are at the party, pull the string and you'll see a surprise for everyone. Love, Mother and Dad.' "

"How wonderful!" said Nan.

It was decided to hang the piñata on the chandelier in the hall. Bert had just put it in place when the bell rang again.

Nellie had arrived. She was carrying a large, flat package.

"What's in it?" Freddie wanted to know.

Nellie took off her snowclothes, then slit the tapes on the package with her fingers, and pulled off the wrapping paper. Inside was a red paper heart with a stiff edge and a frilly white collar.

"Oh, it's cool!" exclaimed Nan. "How did you ever make it?"

"I took a couple of coat hangers and bent them into a heart shape. Then I pasted tissue paper over them and cut up paper doilies to make a lacy rim." She grinned. "It was a pretty gooey job."

"I'll bet it was," Freddie chuckled.

Nan said she had decided to put the heart in the dining room. "We'll hang it from the lamp above the table."

"That's a good idea," said Nellie. "Get some string."

As the two girls carried the heart to the dining room, the young twins spotted Snoop going up the front stairs.

"Let's put a red bow on him for the party," Flossie suggested.

Freddie giggled. "If he'll let us."

Flossie skipped back into the living room and cut a piece of red crepe-paper streamer off the roll she and Nan had been using. Then she and Freddie started quietly up the stairs. By now the big black cat was curled up in a chair in the boys' room. He blinked at them but did not move.

"Here, Snoop," said Flossie in a sweet voice. "Wouldn't you like to get dressed up for the party? Let me put a nice bow around your neck."

As the children approached him, the cat sat up and narrowed his yellow eyes. He did not like the looks of the paper streamer in Flossie's hand.

"Nice kitty," said Freddie, reaching for their pet.

Meow! The cat sprang through Freddie's chubby hands and shot out the door.

"Come back!" cried Flossie. But Snoop wasn't waiting, so the twins raced after him. Down the stairs they went pell-mell.

Meanwhile Nan had taken off her shoes and was standing on a chair beside the dining room table. Nellie handed her the big heart with its frilly lace collar.

"Hold it up, so I can see how the heart will look before you tie it," Nellie requested.

Nan obeyed, and her friend backed toward the door to get a better look at the effect.

Suddenly a loud screech filled the air. Through the door streaked Snoop with the young twins right behind him. Without warning the cat bounded onto the table.

"Stop!" exclaimed Flossie, grabbing for him.

But the frightened cat jumped high into the air. R-rip! Snoop leaped straight through the tissue paper heart!

Nellie gave a wail. Freddie and Flossie looked dismayed. Nan put down the heart and stepped off the chair.

"Oh, Snoop, you naughty, naughty cat," she scolded.

Snoop bounded from the room as fast as he could.

"What made him do that?" Nellie asked.

Flossie and Freddie explained, and Flossie said, "I'm so sorry."

"Never mind," Nellie told her. "I can fix the heart. I brought more red tissue with me. I'm glad the food wasn't spoiled."

The decoration was mended and hung up. Promptly at two o'clock the doorbell rang, and Flossie skipped to open it.

"Susie!" she exclaimed. "You're the very first one except Nellie."

Ten minutes later the party was off to a good start. The younger children played blindman's buff in the basement, while the others had a guessing game in the living room. Prizes were won by Teddy and Ralph Blake.

In a little while Nan called all the children together. "We have two special surprises for you today," she said.

"Two?" the children echoed.

"Make 'em guess," Freddie piped up. He loved guessing games.

"All right," Nan agreed. "Who's first?"

Susie's hand shot up. "We're going to have Valentine ice cream."

"No," Flossie said, giggling. "Who's next?"

Ralph Blake answered. "You'll show us some movies of our school picnic last year."

"That's not right," Bert told him. "But it would be a good idea to do it some time. Anybody else want to guess?"

All the children took a turn except Nellie. None of them was right.

Nan turned to Nellie. "How about you?"

Her friend grinned. "I can't think of two surprises, but does one have to do with the donkey hanging in the hall?"

"It sure does. Good for you, Nellie." Nan explained that the *piñata* held a surprise for each

R-rip! Snoop leaped through the paper heart!

one at the party. "Since Nellie guessed, I think she should be the one to pull the string."

The children crowded around and watched as Nellie's yank on the red ribbon punctured the donkey, and small packages tumbled to the floor.

"Help yourselves," Bert called out, and a great scramble followed.

There was silence for several seconds except for the crackle of tissue as the gifts were unwrapped.

"I got a toy police whistle!" Freddie shouted and blew on it shrilly.

This brought Aunt Sallie on a run from the kitchen. "What's happened? What's the matter?" she cried.

"It's my donkey surprise," Freddie answered.

"Your monkey prize?" Aunt Sallie said. "I thought it sounded more like a whistle." She went back to the kitchen, leaving the children smiling.

There were many kinds of gifts—hair bands, tiny dolls, puzzles, and little books. Some of them had to be transferred from boys to girls. At once everyone began to play with their gifts. Apparently they had forgotten about the second surprise.

Bert whispered to Nan, "When are you going to tell them about the play house?"

"Let's do it while we're eating." Nan looked at the clock. "In five minutes."

She went to the kitchen where Aunt Sallie had hot cocoa waiting. They poured it into cups and put a dab of whipped cream on the top of each. The cups were set on the table, then Nan called the young guests.

As they ate, Susie said, "You never told us what the other surprise is."

Nan smiled. "No, I didn't. How would you all like to become spies? Not make-believe spies, but real ones?"

"Sounds cool," said Charlie. "How do we do it?"

"I'll explain," said Nan. "Then if anybody doesn't want to join the Bobbsey Detective Agency, he won't have to."

Before she had finished telling the plan, everyone was eager to go, and Freddie cried out, "I just got my toy police whistle in time!"

Charlie asked, "How soon after you go, do you want us to start?"

Bert and Nan looked at each other and finally decided that twenty minutes would be good.

"And don't forget, you're not to rush in like a bunch of wild Indians. You're to sneak in two at a time and be quiet like real spies."

"And hide," Susie spoke up. "Nellie, will you go with me?"

"Sure thing."

Teddy Blake said he would stick to his big

brother. "I'll make snowballs and throw them at those bad men."

"No, no," Bert warned. "Your job is to watch and notify Mr. Thurbell. But if the men come to the play house and start to run away, then go after them and throw all the snowballs you want to."

As ice cream was being served, the older twins excused themselves. Bert went for a flashlight and a screwdriver, while Nan got their coats. Then the two hurried off.

"I can hardly wait to see what's in that room!" Nan exclaimed as they ran toward the Springer mansion.

When the twins reached the yard, they heard Rex barking loudly in the garage.

"I guess he's tied there," Bert remarked.

He and his sister hastened down the slope to the play house. Bert tried the front door. It was still locked, so he brought out his key. After the children entered, Bert locked it from the inside.

"I smell soup," Nan said. "Somebody's been eating here." She hurried to the kitchen to look at the stove. There was no sign of food around, but one burner was still warm.

"Maybe this means nobody will come back," Nan remarked.

"Could be," her brother agreed. "Well, there's nothing to see down here. Let's go upstairs."

He led the way to the attic. Nan held the light while her twin unscrewed one of the padlock hasps. As soon as it was off, he opened the door.

The room was dark. As Nan flashed the light around the big closet, both children gasped.

The closet was full of antique toys!

"There's the Chinese mouse cage!" Nan exclaimed.

Bert's eyes were sparkling. "These are probably things Blue bought cheap from the people in Lakeport." He stepped over a kerosene lantern and picked up an old-fashioned fire engine. "I'll bet this is Freddie's—the one Aunt Sallie gave him. It looks just the way he described it."

A moment later he picked up his small brother's stolen hook-and-ladder which had one ladder missing. "Freddie'll be glad to get this back."

"There's Hildy!" Nan suddenly exclaimed. The rag doll lay in a corner. "She looks as if someone threw her there."

Nan stepped over several toys to get Hildy. She stopped short to look at a sign which lay near the doll.

JOHN HARDEN
DEALER IN
ANTIQUE TOYS

"Bert!" she exclaimed. "Look at this! Now we know the answer to the play house mystery.

The man called Hard by Mr. Blue must be Mr. Harden. He *is* here—at least now, even if he isn't living in the big house."

Bert nodded. "He must be in partnership with Mr. Blue, who's stealing antique toys or buying them real cheap like giving Freddie only a dollar for this nifty fire engine."

As he spoke, Bert turned over the fire engine. On the bottom were the words HARDEN ANTIQUE TOYS stamped in blue ink. Nan picked up the mouse cage and looked at the bottom of it. The same stamp. Bert examined a few other toys. All had Harden's name on them.

Bert looked determined. "We'd better lock up now and get the police."

But as the twins turned toward the door they stopped in their tracks. There were men's voices outside, and a key was being fitted into the front door lock!

"We're too late!" Nan whispered. "It isn't time yet for the other children to come. We're trapped!"

CHAPTER XVIII

VALENTINE DETECTIVE PARTY

"WHAT shall we do?" Nan whispered, frightened.

Heavy footsteps sounded from below as two men entered the play house. The door closed.

Bert touched his sister's arm and gestured her back into the attic closet. The children tiptoed across the floor. Bert put out his flashlight and quietly shut the door.

"Maybe they won't come up here," he said softly. "Anyhow, we have no choice."

"If only Freddie and Flossie and the others would come!" thought Nan.

The rumble of voices came to the twins' ears. Bert and Nan knelt quietly beside a wide crack in the floor. They could see the two men standing in a corner of the living room. Blue and Harden!

"Get the list and hurry up," Harden growled.

Blue pulled a black notebook from his pocket.

He handed it to his employer. Harden carefully examined several pages.

"Good!" he said. "An antique fire engine for one dollar. Not bad at all!"

"And the Chinese mouse cage," Blue added eagerly. "Look at what I paid for it, Hard."

"I can get ten times that much money," the big man said. For a few minutes he made notes in the book, then showed it to Blue. "See the prices I put next to those toys? Sky high! That's how I got rich!"

"Don't people catch on to the scheme?" Blue asked.

Harden grunted. "Sure. That's why I had to leave Florida." Suddenly his voice grew stern. "Now that we've got time, suppose you explain how you bungled over the Chinese cage."

"I told you," said Blue hoarsely. "The old lady mixed up the two packages."

"So what? Why didn't you just go to the Bobbseys' house and ask for your own box?"

"Because I was afraid, that's why," Blue replied. "Do you think I want to be connected with that cage? Suppose the Villey woman found out she'd been cheated and complained to the police? I've been working this area for a couple of weeks, and I was nervous. I even brought a little tank of gas down here for cooking on the stove in case I had to hide out in the play house."

Harden gave a mean laugh. "You're scared of your own shadow, Blue!"

"You don't know what I went through with those Bobbseys!" his employee replied. "I remember the first day I saw them. I'd slipped into the mansion to see if there was any place I could hide the crates of toys you sent from Florida."

Blue told about watching from a second floor window as the dog jumped on Flossie. "Little did I know what trouble those twins would make for me. I guess I should have locked this house," he went on, "but nobody ever came around here, so I didn't. Besides, I padlocked the attic. That was the important place.

"One day I came to put some toys up there and found a doll in the rocker. I took it to the attic, figuring that when the child found it was gone, she'd be afraid to play here any more. Then I looked out the window and saw that little Bobbsey girl and another kid coming, so I moaned to frighten them away.

"But the twins just didn't scare," Blue went on. "The girls even came back for a party. After that I locked the play house."

"You ought to be ashamed of yourself," Harden said. "Afraid of a bunch of kids!"

"But nothing stops them," Blue complained. "When the window in their attic banged in the wind they came right up to investigate. I just had time to fasten it and hide in the wardrobe.

"One time the two girls were looking for their kitten and nearly caught me in the attic, but I played ghost and got away."

"What were you doing up there?" Harden asked.

"I came to get back my green scarf, so it couldn't be used as evidence against me. One of their little friends had grabbed it off my neck the day I ran away from here."

"You're so stupid sometimes," Harden said. "But anyhow you got the scarf back and picked up an old hook-and-ladder besides. But you've got the police after us.

"When I think how careful I've been to keep this scheme a secret! I planned to hold the loot in the attic closet here for a while. Then I was going to alter the toys a little so people wouldn't recognize what they had sold. Afterwards I'd put them into my stock.

"I came up quietly from Florida to look over the situation and registered at the Happy Traveler Motel under a false name. What did I find? Children chasing you. I sure ought to fire you, even if you are my cousin! Now show me that Chinese mouse cage," he added harshly.

The twins' hearts pounded as the men moved out of sight and heavy footsteps mounted the ladder. If only the other children would come!

The next moment there was a muffled exclamation, as the men saw the padlock hanging. The door was pulled open. Blue and Harden came in.

Blue stared, open-mouthed, but Harden's face grew dark red with fury. "I'm going to teach you snoopy kids a lesson," he declared. As he stepped toward the twins, suddenly they heard the sound of children's voices below.

"Nan! Bert! Are you all right?" called Flossie.

"It's the Valentine party!" exclaimed Nan. "They're here!"

As the men stared at each other, dumfounded, Bert shouted, "Freddie! Call the police! Hurry!"

"We already did!"

"Get out quick!" yelled Harden to his cousin.

The men tore down the ladder with the twins after them.

"Catch those men!" Bert shouted to his friends.

"Out of my way!" cried Harden.

He thrust several children aside as he burst through the door of the play house with Blue at his heels. They were greeted with a rain of snowballs thrown by the young spies!

Yelling, a dozen boys and girls raced after the

men. Bert sprinted way ahead of them and dashed into the garage. Quickly he untied the dog.

"Come on, Rex," he said, "I need you!"

They ran out together, as the men raced over the top of the slope, their coats flapping.

"Stop 'em, Rex!" cried Bert.

When the big dog bounded toward the fleeing men, they turned back and met the Valentine party head on.

"Surround them!" cried Nan, and the children formed a ring around the men, the dog, and Bert.

"Break through!" shouted Harden desperately.

He and Blue made a rush, but Bert and Charlie tripped them. The men fell in the deep snow and the circle closed tighter. The dog stood growling over the thieves. The next moment Mr. Thurbell raced from the mansion.

"Let us go! It's all a mistake!" cried Harden.

The caretaker looked straight at the two men. "We'll wait until the police come," he said. "They're on the way."

A few minutes later a siren wailed, and a squad car drove into the back yard. Four officers piled out and led the shivering men to the living room of the mansion. The others, including Rex, followed.

All the children except the Bobbseys looked

The young spies sent a rain of snowballs

around curiously at the furniture. It was covered with white plastic sheets. Officer Lane ordered the two men to sit on the sofa.

"Now then," he said, "let's have the story."

Bert and Nan told all they had seen and heard. When they reached the part about the toys in the play house, one officer slipped out of the room.

"A record of all the frauds," Bert said, "is in a little black book in Mr. Harden's pocket."

"And in Mr. Blue's pocket," Nan added, "you may find the bell he took off the cage to make it seem damaged."

"You may as well hand them over now," said Officer Lane sternly.

Glaring at Nan, the men obeyed.

Mr. Thurbell spoke up coldly. "Mr. Harden, I guess you won't be living here after all. If you want to sell this dog, I'll buy him. All right?" Harden nodded grimly.

In a few minutes the other officer returned carrying Hildy. "The toys are all there, just as the children say," he reported and handed the rag doll to Flossie. "This one isn't evidence, so you can have her."

"Oh, thank you!" the little girl exclaimed, hugging Hildy tightly.

Freddie stepped forward and pulled a dollar bill from his pocket. He handed it to Blue.

"Here's your money back," he said. "I'll take my engine, and my hook-and-ladder too."

"Later, Freddie," said Officer Lane. "We'll need them now to show at the trial."

Blue groaned. "You Bobbseys were our undoing!"

"You did a fine job, children," said Officer Lane. Mr. Thurbell joined in the praise, and the Valentine party cheered.

"Everybody helped," said Bert.

Charlie grinned. "This sure was a cool Valentine party."

Nellie winked at Nan. "I loved being a spy."

"Me too! Me too!" echoed the others.

As the police led the prisoners away the children said good-by to Mr. Thurbell and headed for their various homes.

"Let's stop at the vet's and see if Snap is well," Nan suggested to her brothers and sister.

Twenty minutes later the dog was trotting down the street beside them, his tail waving in the air.

"Look!" whooped Freddie as they neared their home. "Mother and Daddy are back!" He pointed to the station wagon standing in the drive. Shouting, the twins ran into the house with Snap barking at their heels.

Mr. and Mrs. Bobbsey were in the front hall, taking off their coats. The twins threw themselves into their parents' arms and for a few minutes everyone was hugging and kissing and talking at once.

"Welcome back!" came Aunt Sallie's voice and she walked in from the kitchen. "How is your Uncle Ross?"

"Much, much better, thank you," said Mrs. Bobbsey. "Did you have fun?" she asked the children.

"Yes, and lots of mysteries," Bert answered.

"Oh, Mother," Nan exclaimed, "we had wonderful adventures at the play house!"

Aunt Sallie looked surprised. "Playing with a mouse! Who was doing that?" Then she rolled her eyes. "To think I never knew a thing about it!"